**Look for other Sealed Mysteries
by Ann Evans:**

For our very own little Jake.
And for my brother Eddie Carroll – thanks, Ted!

Scholastic Children's Books
Commonwealth House, 1–19 New Oxford Street,
London WC1A 1NU, UK
London ~ New York ~ Toronto ~ Sydney ~ Auckland
Mexico City ~ New Delhi ~ Hong Kong
First published by Scholastic Ltd, 2000

Text copyright © Ann Evans, 2000

ISBN 0 439 01148 5

Typeset by M Rules
Printed by Cox & Wyman Ltd, Reading, Berks

10 9 8 7 6 5 4 3 2 1

The right of Ann Evans to be identified as the author of this work has been
asserted by her in accordance with the Copyright, Designs and Patents Act, 1988.

1

"If we're going to bump into a dead body on this boat," Candy Everton announced, following her dad and younger brother, Jake, along the canal towpath, "I'm not getting on to it!"

"Not again!" her dad groaned. "I keep telling you, no one has died. The original owner simply abandoned the *Baloo*. The canal authorities finally claimed her and they've sold her to me. It's all perfectly legal."

"And creepy," Candy grumbled, not liking the idea at all. "I can't understand why anyone would just abandon their narrowboat. Why not sell it if they didn't want it any more? Why desert it? Doesn't make sense to me."

"Questions, questions," Mr Everton laughed as they trudged along the dusty track. "She's ours now and that's official. And once we've spruced her up she'll look magnificent."

"Hey! Is that it?" Jake yelled as they entered a long, low brick tunnel spanning the canal.

At the far end of the tunnel, framed beneath the dark archway of brick, a long green narrowboat was moored to the bank, looking neglected and forgotten.

"That's her," Mr Everton sighed happily. "The *Baloo* – and she's all mine at last."

Jake ran on ahead, making loud whooping noises that echoed around the damp, arched brickwork. Reaching the far end of the tunnel he called back, "It's a bit scruffy."

"You'd be scruffy if no one had looked after you for over a year," Candy shouted. Then, grinning, she added, "Actually, you already are a bit scruffy."

Jake stuck out his tongue and clambered aboard the *Baloo*.

"Hang on," Mr Everton yelled, quickening his step. "Life jackets at all times, please."

He pulled out three bright yellow life jackets from his holdall and they slipped them on over their T-shirts. "Can't take any chances. The water's deep."

"And murky," Candy murmured, peering down into the muddy brown depths.

Mr Everton ran his hand along the peeling paintwork of the *Baloo*. "Well, kids, what do you reckon? Think your mum will like her?"

Candy stood back from the water's edge and gazed at the narrowboat. Despite the grime and the flaky paintwork, she could see that it had once been beautiful and that someone had taken infinite care over decorating it. Below the layers of dirt were painted scenes of castles, roses, boats and rivers, intricately designed and painted with love and care.

Mr Everton gazed happily at the boat. "Y'know, kids, I've always wanted this boat. First spotted her years ago, when you two were just babies."

"Did you meet the owner?" Candy asked, more puzzled than ever now she'd seen the boat. Why would anyone abandon something they so obviously treasured?

"Met him once," her dad remarked, thinking

back. "Big chap as I recall, with a bushy black beard. Quite an artist too: painted all these scenes himself."

"Canal art," Jake piped up, sitting perched on a wooden bench seat at the rear of the boat and waggling the long tiller back and forth. "We've done it at school. Can we go below now, Dad?"

Mr Everton stepped on board, taking a set of keys tied to a chunk of wood from his holdall. "Good idea, eh?" he remarked. "If you drop the keys overboard, they'll float."

Candy followed him, gripping the rail with both hands. The *Baloo* dipped in the water. It was a strange, unsettling sensation and she hoped the boat was still watertight.

The cabin door was small, and they had to duck as they went down the two steps into the galley. There was a cold, dark chill to the long narrow cabin. The curtains were shut. Everything looked shadowy and unwelcoming.

Candy felt as if she were trespassing. As if the previous owner was still there, somewhere. Watching them. Angry that they were intruding on *his* boat.

Mr Everton opened the curtains and the August sunlight streaked in. The boat was furnished with a table and bench seats. At the far end, near the door which opened up on to the bow, were four bunk beds, two either side. There were cupboards, a sink, a cooker and a cast iron wood stove with a chimney that went out through the roof.

"Well, what do you think?" he asked, smiling broadly.

"Brilliant!" declared Jake, poking about in the cupboards. "Except there's a load of junk everywhere."

"It wants a good clearing out," his dad remarked.

Candy gazed around, holding on to the sink to keep her balance as the boat bobbed about on the water. It was quite pretty really, beneath all the dust. Every wall and door was decorated with canal art, bright pictures in reds, greens and yellows. Even the pots and pans were painted.

"Look," she said, glancing at a bright red kettle sitting on old newspapers on the table. "He was halfway through painting a scene on this kettle."

Jake jabbed a rock-hard paintbrush on the tabletop. "All his paints have dried up."

Candy frowned. There was a mug and plate on the table too, and half a loaf of bread which was now just a lump of hard green mould. What looked like the skeleton of a fish lay dried up on the plate next to a knife and fork. An unwashed saucepan sat on the cooker. A pile of ruffled bedclothes lay untidily on the top bunk.

"It looks as if he abandoned the *Baloo* in a hurry," she murmured, glancing around the galley.

"He's even left his clothes and shoes," announced Jake, opening another cupboard. "Pooh! And his socks." He shut the cupboard door quickly and opened the next. "Hey, look at this!"

"What have you found?" his dad asked, stooping down to take a look.

"Bottles of booze – brandy! Loads of it."

Mr Everton picked up one of the fat brown bottles and read the label. "Mmm, excellent brand and pretty rare. Can't buy it in this country. It must have come from the Continent. You wouldn't leave this behind unless you had to."

"See?" Candy murmured. "I told you it was odd."

Jake continued delving through the cupboards. "This one's stuffed full of papers, letters and things. Hey, was his name Benjamin Fisher?'

"Yes, I believe so," said Mr Everton. "Just throw it all away. I've brought plenty of rubbish sacks."

But Candy was still puzzled. Why leave everything behind like this? Clothes, letters, all that brandy. . . He was halfway through painting a picture on a kettle. He hadn't washed up his dinner plate. It was just so odd.

Jake sniffed at a green piece of mould that had once been a slice of bread and butter and waggled the dried-up fish bones at Candy. "Mmm, nice. Fancy a sandwich?"

"No, you eat it," she answered, smiling sweetly. But her smile soon turned to a frown. "He must have gone out after his dinner and had an accident or something. It's so sad."

"It certainly looks that way," her dad agreed. "But these things happen. Bad luck for Benjamin Fisher, but good for us. I've always wanted to own the *Baloo*," he gazed around the boat, smiling happily, "and now I do."

"But aren't you bothered about what

happened to him?" Candy insisted. "This was his last meal. That was his last painting. . ." her gaze turned to the bundle of bedclothes. "It even looks like he'd been in bed. . ."

Her heart lurched. There was a definite *shape* to those bedclothes. An icy shiver crawled up her spine. "Dad . . . you don't think. . .?"

A look of horror spread across Mr Everton's face. "Died in his sleep, you mean? And no one discovered him?"

Jake's brown eyes looked like saucers. He backed away from the bunks.

"Have a look, Dad," Candy whispered, grabbing hold of Jake and holding him close.

Mr Everton looked distinctly nervous. "Don't be so daft. Someone would have checked . . . wouldn't they?"

"Maybe not," Candy breathed. "Make sure, Dad – go on."

He hesitated nervously. "It's just bedclothes."

"It might not be," Candy whispered, her skin beginning to crawl with horror.

Slowly, very slowly, Mr Everton inched along the galley towards the bunk bed. Cautiously, his hand reached out towards the bundle of bedclothes.

Candy and Jake held their breath.

Gripping the edges of the grey woollen blankets, Mr Everton yanked them clean off the bed with a loud "Waahh!"

Candy and Jake screamed.

A second later their dad was doubled up with laughter. "You pair of nits! You didn't really think old Benjamin Fisher was still lying in his bed? Give me a bit of credit, please."

Candy gave her dad a thump. "You did that just to scare us, didn't you? You've already checked the boat over, haven't you?"

"Course I have. Honestly, you pair!" he grinned. "Now let's get some work done."

Candy glared. "That wasn't funny. I nearly had a heart attack."

"*I* wasn't scared," Jake shrugged, the colour returning to his cheeks.

"No, I could see that," Candy remarked knowingly.

"I wasn't!"

Candy heaved a sigh as she looked all around. "So, where shall we start?"

"Wherever you like," her dad replied, still chuckling to himself. "But watch out for the dead bodies."

Candy pulled a face at him as she tugged the brass handle of a long, thin door. "What's in here anyway?"

"That's the toilet," said her dad. "I haven't looked in there yet. So if Benjamin Fisher is still aboard, he could be sitting on the loo."

"Very funny," said Candy, smiling sweetly and giving the door a pull.

It opened suddenly.

It was a tiny little room. There was just enough room for someone to squeeze in, sit down . . . and die.

For there, sitting on the loo, pipe stuck between his bony jaws, spectacles dangling from hollow eye sockets, trousers round his ankles and an old newspaper on his lap . . . was the skeleton of Benjamin Fisher.

Rigid with shock, Candy could only stand there, staring. Eventually Jake wandered over and peered over her shoulder.

Candy had never realized until then just how loudly her little brother could scream.

2

When Jake's high-pitched shriek had stopped ringing in Candy's ears, she heard something else.

Someone laughing.

The children spun round to find their father holding on to his sides, tears rolling down his cheeks.

"I might have known!" Candy groaned. "You put it there. It's a joke shop skeleton, isn't it? Relax, Jake, it's not real."

Jake gave a shrug. "I knew that. Didn't scare me."

"Oh sure," Candy remarked. "You thought you'd perforate my eardrums just for fun."

Jake pulled a face and busied himself with the drawers and cupboards crammed full of Benjamin Fisher's possessions.

"Realistic, isn't he?" his dad grinned, wobbling the skeleton's jaw up and down. "Couldn't resist winding you two up, seeing as you've been harping on and on about the owner disappearing ever since I told you I was buying the *Baloo*."

"Well, he *has* disappeared, you can't deny that," Candy argued.

"People abandon boats all the time," Mr Everton explained. "They lose interest, or can't afford to renew their licence, so they abandon them. Eventually the canal authorities move in, put a notice on the boat warning the owner to get in touch or they claim the boat, then sell it."

"Well, I still think it's odd," Candy grumbled.

"Odd or not," said her dad, giving her a hug, "Benjamin Fisher isn't around any more. The *Baloo* is ours, and we've got three days to get her shipshape before your mum comes aboard for inspection. So let's get cracking."

Candy glanced warily at the thick cobwebs around the little windows. "We're not really going to sleep here tonight, are we?"

"We certainly are. Got to make the most of my bank holiday weekend. It's all right for you with your six-week summer break, but I've got work on Tuesday."

"Just think of the holidays we can have!" Jake exclaimed excitedly.

"It's going to be great," agreed his dad. "But first we've got to clean her up, so. . ." He pushed a broom into Candy's hand and a roll of plastic sacks into Jake's. "Jake, you throw away all the rubbish. Candy, sweep the main decks. Any mutiny and you'll be a-walkin' the plank. Ah-ha, Jim lad!"

Candy and Jake exchanged glances and smiled sympathetically at their dad. Giving them a jaunty wink, he donned his captain's cap and went up on deck to make a start on the engine.

"I wish he'd washed his supper things before he disappeared," Candy remarked, gingerly throwing away the mouldy cup and plate. "Do you think he ate a lot of fish? Living on a canal like this."

"He certainly collected some rubbish," Jake groaned, sifting through some drawers. "Shall I chuck out these old bills and his diary?"

Candy stared at her brother. "You've found his diary? Is it written in?"

"Every day by the look of it," Jake muttered, flicking through the pages.

Candy stared at the battered old notebook. "Jake . . . that diary might give us a clue as to where he went."

Jake's eyes opened wide. "Candy, I'm shocked! You're not thinking of reading someone else's diary, are you? Not you – the girl who went bananas when you caught me reading yours."

"That was different," Candy glared. "This might tell us something important."

Before Jake could argue, his dad came below deck again. "Jake, you haven't come across an engine manual, have you?"

"Mmm, I think I did. Hang on," Jake muttered, sifting through the junk. "Is this it?"

He pushed aside the dried-up pots of paints and brushes and the kettle which Benjamin Fisher had been painting his last canal scene on, to retrieve a dog-eared, greasy engine manual.

"Ah-ha!" beamed his dad. "Now let's see how the carburettor works."

As he studied the manual Candy and Jake got on with their tidying. Candy was itching to look at the diary. The fact that Benjamin Fisher had left it behind just added to the mystery. It could hold a vital clue as to why he had vanished into thin air.

Suddenly the narrowboat dipped, as if someone had jumped on deck. Wide-eyed, Candy hissed, "Who's that?"

They stood motionless, listening, feeling the boat bob about in the water.

Then came a shout.

"Ben! Benjamin, is that you?"

They all jumped as a face peered round the cabin doorway, blocking the sunlight. "Oh, sorry!" it said.

It was a pleasant face. A smooth, sun-tanned complexion. A sweatband clamping his fair hair to his head. Bright blue eyes.

"Can I help you?" Mr Everton asked the young man, as they all trooped up on deck to see who it was.

He was wearing running shorts, a T-shirt and trainers. Breathing hard and sweating profusely, he apologized again.

"Sorry, didn't mean to intrude. Only the

Baloo's been standing empty so long. Took me by surprise to see her opened up again. I thought Benjamin was back. Friends of his, are you?"

"Us? No," said Mr Everton. "We're the new owners."

"New owners?" the young man repeated, his face dropping. "Ben's not coming back then? Don't suppose you know where he went, do you?"

"Sorry, haven't a clue."

"Did you know him well?" Candy asked curiously.

"Well? No, not *well*," the runner replied quickly. A little too quickly. As if he suddenly didn't want to be associated with Benjamin Fisher. Then he relaxed and smiled. "Always said good morning or afternoon to each other on my runs. It's a hobby of mine, running. I always come along by the canal when my shifts allow."

"Shifts?" Candy asked, puzzled.

"My work," he explained, starting to jog on the spot, making the boat sway to and fro. "Long-distance lorry driver on the Continent. All that sitting – that's why I like to go running when I get the chance."

Mr Everton pushed his captain's cap to the back of his head. "The kids are really curious as to what happened to the old owner. You've no idea?"

"No, that's why I asked you. Maybe he just wanted out."

"Out of what?" Jake asked, frowning.

The runner gave them a half-hearted smile. "Out of a situation. Out of this way of life. Maybe he wanted a change of scene. Who knows? Ah! Morning, Mrs Ellis."

Everyone turned.

A postwoman was heading their way. A short, chunky woman in flat shoes with a scowl on her face. Her small beady eyes flicked disapprovingly over each of them in turn.

"Morning," she replied curtly. "Don't tell me that old nuisance is back?"

"No, afraid not," the runner answered, hiding a smile. "These are the new owners of the *Baloo*."

The stout little woman, her skirt flapping around her knees, looked them up and down. "New owners, eh? Well, let's hope you keep yourselves to yourselves and don't poke your noses into what doesn't concern you!"

She stalked off, disappearing into a small grey stone cottage set back from the canal. The slamming of the door caused a duck to take flight.

"Friendly lady!" Mr Everton chuckled.

The runner lowered his voice. "I shouldn't really tell you. Benjamin swore me to secrecy, but. . ."

"What?" begged Candy.

He lowered his voice to a whisper. "Benjamin once spotted her burning a load of mail because she was too lazy to deliver it."

"No!" gasped Candy, wondering if that was why she'd never heard from that competition she'd entered last year. They didn't live that far from the canal. She could have been their post-woman!

"Benjamin tackled her about it. Said he was going to report her," the runner continued, his eyes sparkling. "She really hated old Ben."

"And did he report her?" Candy asked, glaring at the cottage where the lazy postwoman lived. There'd been a prize of ten CDs for that competition.

"He couldn't have; she's still got her job, hasn't she? Anyway, I'd better be off. Be seeing you." And with a cheery wave, he sprinted off along the towpath.

Feeling decidedly annoyed, Candy perched herself up on the wooden bench seat by the tiller. Fancy burning mail – other people's mail! Benjamin Fisher *should* have reported her.

With a sigh, she gazed over the long green roof of the narrowboat to where the canal disappeared into the tunnel. Although the water was brown and murky, there was a certain beauty to all this.

Nearby was an old inn – *The King Edward* – which sold hot home-made food, so the sign said. Alongside it were two old cottages – the postwoman's and one converted into a little shop. Way off in the opposite direction was a big iron bridge which spanned the canal. And through it Candy could spy the locks and the lock-keeper's cottage.

It was all so peaceful. How strange that Benjamin Fisher had abandoned all this. And it was such a beautiful boat – or at least it had been. On its roof stood potted plants, their flowers now withered and dead. But the pots were painted so cheerfully, each with its own little canal scene framed by roses and castles.

Candy peered closer at one of the flowerpots. Benjamin Fisher had painted a picture of the iron bridge and a boat passing beneath it. The boat looked just like the *Baloo*, and there was a man on board.

She smiled wistfully. Benjamin had painted himself in the picture.

"Coming up the front end?" Jake called to her, teetering like a tight-rope walker on the little ledge that ran along the sides of the boat.

"It's called the bow," Mr Everton corrected him as Candy followed her brother. "And be careful. You're all right where we're moored, but if you slip off the gunnel on the other side, you're in deep water."

Candy balanced her way along the gunnel to the front of the *Baloo*. Then, sitting on the wooden slats of the bow, she gazed lazily down into the canal.

A tangle of ropes and fenders dangled down into the muddy brown water. And merged with the confusion of ropes and weights lying just below the rippling surface, her reflection stared back up at her.

The water looked dark, black almost. Uninviting.

She shivered.

Suddenly there was a commotion. Loud music blaring. Shouts and shrieks and laughter. Candy looked up to find a large narrowboat heading straight for them – at top speed.

"Dad!" Candy yelled.

"Hang on to something kids – it's going to hit us!" Mr Everton yelled, frantically waving his arms at the rowdy crew. Snatching up the bargepole, he tried to push the oncoming boat away. "Move over, you fools – you're going to ram us!"

Candy and Jake clung on to the sides of the *Baloo*, bracing themselves for the impact.

At the last second, the speeding craft veered slightly and Mr Everton managed to push it further away with the bargepole so that it only grazed them. But the near crash sent the *Baloo* rocking and swaying violently and a surge of water came splashing over the sides.

"You idiots!" Mr Everton shouted at the laughing bunch of teenagers as they sped past.

The *Baloo* took some minutes to stop rocking. The wake from the other narrowboat had churned and dredged up the sludge from the depths.

Green slime rose to the surface. A bicycle wheel floated to the top and spun crazily, as if it were being powered by an underwater cyclist. There was other rubbish too. Candy stared in disgust at the pile of old clothing tangled in ropes that surfaced and floated alongside the *Baloo*.

"Honestly, the things people throw into canals. . ." Her voice faded away.

The pile of old clothing was taking on a distinct form.

Trousers, a shirt – its arms outstretched. Gloves – grey-white gloves. Only they weren't gloves – they were hands.

And then a face. A face which bobbed up and out of the black, swirling depths. Not much of a face, but a face none the less. With a black beard. With hair. But a sightless face that was long, long dead.

"Dad. . ." Candy croaked, knowing she would have to find a louder voice if she wanted to make him hear.

"Dad," she tried again. "Dad, I think I know what happened to Benjamin Fisher. . ."

3

As soon as their dad saw the body in the water, he ordered Candy and Jake off the boat while he ran to phone the police from the nearby *King Edward Inn.*

As the children stood trembling on the towpath, a handful of people came hurrying from the inn to see for themselves. They stood on the edge of the bank and peered around the boat, pointing and whispering. A fisherman who had been sitting just a little way up the canal wandered down to join them, a puzzled look on his face. The postwoman emerged from her cottage, grumbling at all the noise.

"What's going on, landlord?" the fisherman asked a stout red-faced man, whose wife, equally as stout, had come running from *The King Edward Inn* and was clinging on to him, a handkerchief pressed to her mouth.

"These folk have found a body in the water," said the landlord, patting the woman's hand comfortingly. "Stay here, Kath. I'll take a look."

He climbed aboard the *Baloo* and peered into the canal on the far side of the boat. A few moments later he glanced back and nodded his head sadly.

With a great wail, the woman burst into tears and stood sobbing noisily into her handkerchief.

"Let me see," the postwoman grumbled, hitching up her skirt and stepping aboard the *Baloo*. She stood next to the landlord, staring down. They were both there a long time. When she finally turned away from the awful sight in the water there was a strange expression on her face – a kind of smug, self-satisfied look.

Candy gave Jake a nudge and hissed, "Look at her! What's she looking so pleased about?"

"Maybe she pushed him," Jake hissed back. "She looks pretty pleased about something."

"That's him all right," the postwoman

announced to everyone on the towpath. "That's Benjamin Fisher. Probably fell overboard drunk. Serves him right."

The landlady of the pub stopped her sniffling and glared furiously at the postwoman. "How can you speak ill of the dead? Benjamin was a decent man. He was always fair. He never cheated us—"

"Sshh, Kath," the landlord stopped her, jumping off the *Baloo* and hurrying to her side. Warning signs were flashing from his bulging eyes. There was a secret here – a secret they didn't want to share.

She shut up immediately.

Candy gave Jake another nudge. "What did she mean by that – Benjamin never cheated them? They must have been involved in something."

Jake shrugged. "Cheated at cards maybe?"

Keeping her voice low, Candy murmured, "So what are they whispering about now? Just look at them. They're up to something."

Mr Everton returned from phoning the police. He wrapped his arms around Candy and Jake. "Police are on their way, and so is the lock-keeper. The police said they'd contact him right away."

"Here he comes now," the landlord said, nodding in the direction of the lock-keeper's cottage. Someone was just coming out of the door and breaking into a run.

Mr Everton glanced around the small crowd. "Does anyone know who he was?"

The landlady immediately started to sob again.

"It's Benjamin Fisher," the landlord said softly. "He used to own the *Baloo*."

The fisherman, a puny little man with a small moustache and frightened eyes, asked nervously, "Are you sure it's Benjamin?"

"Take a look for yourself," the postwoman snapped unkindly.

The fisherman backed even further away from the water's edge. "Oh no . . . no, I won't . . . I couldn't. How do you think it happened? Just fell, did he?"

"Drunk!" the postwoman pronounced, arms folded and lips pursed.

The pub landlady moved forward angrily and her husband held her back.

Candy glanced at the timid fisherman. His face had turned a sickly shade of grey. "Was he your friend?" she asked him gently.

He was trembling and biting his nails. He had delicate hands, with gold rings on both little fingers. He wore an expensive-looking gold watch too. "Pardon? Oh yes, a friend . . . sort of. . ."

"I'm so sorry," Candy said, hoping to comfort him. He looked as if he might dissolve into a quivering heap on the floor at any second.

"You – you've bought the *Baloo* then," the fisherman continued. "I saw you arriving earlier. I fish here a lot. Most days since I . . . er . . . retired."

"Yes," replied Mr Everton. "We're just getting rid of the cobwebs."

"It's been standing empty a long time, well over a year," the fisherman went on, his eyes darting everywhere. "I – I wonder what the police will do."

"Fish him out, I suppose," Jake said bluntly.

Candy dug him in the ribs. The fisherman began biting his nails again. Candy wanted to tell him not to. He had such nice nails, well manicured. This must have really upset him.

"Do – do you think they'll bring in the frogmen?" he asked anxiously.

"Possibly," Mr Everton shrugged.

The lock-keeper arrived then, puffing from his run along the towpath. He was a tall, broad shouldered man, well into his sixties. His hair and beard were grey, speckled with the last traces of black from his youth. He had sharp eyes and a hard, rugged look that told of years working outdoors in all weathers.

He took charge of the situation immediately. "Stand back," he said in a gruff voice, as he looked all around the boat.

Candy wanted to tell him the body couldn't be seen from the towpath and that he'd have to get on board and look over the other side. But he looked so self assured, she decided he would work that out for himself, and so she stood silently, like everyone else.

Moments later he stepped aboard and nimbly walked the length of the gunnel to the bow and crouched down. Everyone waited silently on the towpath. No one spoke. It was as if they were all holding their breath. Waiting. As if the lock-keeper could make it all right. As if he could bring Benjamin back to life.

He was a long while just staring down into the water.

Candy snuggled closer to her dad. She felt

shivery despite the warm August sunshine. "How can he keep staring?" she whispered finally.

Eventually the lock-keeper jumped from the *Baloo* back on to the towpath and stood there with his chest puffed out. On his crisp white shirt he wore a badge bearing the words "Lock-Keeper, Leadbury Junction".

"That's Benjamin Fisher!" he announced unnecessarily. "Owner of the *Baloo*. God rest his soul."

"*Previous* owner," Mr Everton interrupted, so that everyone turned and stared.

"Dad!" Candy hissed, embarrassed.

The lock-keeper raised one bushy white eyebrow. "Aye, beg pardon. Previous owner."

"Do you think they'll bring in the frogmen?" the fisherman asked again, his small eyes wide and frightened.

"Aye, probably," the lock-keeper answered stiffly, standing there looking very important.

The fisherman's knees seemed to buckle.

At that moment the runner who had spoken to the Evertons came jogging back along the path. He skidded to a halt at the sight of the crowd. "Hello, what's happened here?"

Before anyone could tell him, the pub landlord and landlady dragged him to one side and began talking in whispers.

Candy glanced at Jake. "Secret society!" she hissed.

The lock-keeper cleared his throat, and stood waiting for everyone to fall silent. He looked as if he was used to dealing with dead bodies.

"All right, everybody, the excitement's over. Authorities have been informed. I suggest you all go about your business."

The landlady dissolved into floods of tears again. Wrenching free from her husband's arms she marched straight up to the lock-keeper. "I don't know how you can stand there like that, Ted Johnstone. That's your old pal lying drowned. You've known Benjamin longer than any of us, and you haven't even shed a tear!"

"Tears are shed in the privacy of one's own home," he answered, unruffled, staring away over her head. "Now why don't you go indoors? Like I say, excitement's over."

"He's right, Kath. Let's go in," the landlord agreed, taking his wife's plump elbow. But she shrugged him off and stood, twisting her hand-kerchief anxiously.

Once more the lock-keeper stepped on board the *Baloo*, as if the sight fascinated him. Again, he peered down at Benjamin Fisher.

Candy watched him, curious as to why he wasn't upset if he had known Benjamin such a long time. And then her curiosity deepened to distrust.

As the lock-keeper turned away from Benjamin, floating there in his watery grave, Candy saw the expression on his face. It was a look of pure satisfaction!

The moment passed instantly, but it left Candy feeling shaken. Had she imagined it? Or was the lock-keeper actually glad that Benjamin was dead?

And it wasn't just him. The postwoman stood there, arms folded, her face hard. Another one glad that Benjamin was dead and gone.

The lock-keeper spoke up again. "Benjamin Fisher is sadly no longer with us," he reminded everyone in a loud voice, as if they needed reminding. "Everything that Benjamin ever knew, or was, has gone with him. Every last secret has gone, never to return."

What a strange thing to say. And there! That

look of satisfaction again! Candy thought. He *was* glad that Benjamin was dead. But why?

"Not completely," Jake remarked.

Everyone swung round. Sharp, hostile eyes stared inquisitively. An unnerving silence and stillness descended.

"He left a diary, that's all I was going to say," Jake said simply. "Benjamin Fisher left a diary."

Nobody moved. Nobody uttered a word or breathed or murmured, yet the atmosphere was so hostile, you could feel it.

Candy moved to her brother's side and put her arm protectively around his shoulders. They stared back at all the unfriendly faces.

The discovery of Benjamin Fisher's body had come as a shock to everyone, but the fact that he had kept a diary seemed to have shocked them even more.

Candy couldn't wait to read it!

4

Reading Benjamin's diary, however, would have to wait. Minutes later the police arrived and everyone was ushered inside *The King Edward Inn* while the grizzly task of removing Benjamin's body from the canal was undertaken.

"Stiff brandies all round, I think," said the landlord as he led the way into the inn. "Brandy's good for shock."

"What would the children like?" the landlady asked, still sniffing.

"Coke, please," said Jake.

"Me too, please," added Candy, looking

around. It was a quaint old inn with a cobbled floor and horse-brasses all around the timbered beams.

The landlord poured brandies for the adults from a fat brown bottle. Candy recognized it as being the same sort Benjamin had stored in his cupboard. She nudged her dad and told him.

"So it is," Mr Everton agreed, accepting his glass of brandy from the landlord and sipping it. "Thank you, landlord. Phew! This is strong stuff. It's the same brand as Benjamin Fisher's got stashed away on his boat, isn't it? I gather someone went abroad for their holidays and brought a supply back?"

"Yes, just a few bottles for special occasions," said the landlord, only to be contradicted at the same second by his wife.

"No!" she spluttered, then, glancing awkwardly at her husband, she turned bright pink and apologized. "Oh, sorry, I mean, yes. Yes, we did. I'm so upset by all this, I just can't think straight."

"That's understandable," agreed Mr Everton sympathetically. "It's bad enough for us and we didn't even know Benjamin Fisher."

"It's dreadful!" the landlady murmured,

searching for her handkerchief again. "Just dreadful."

Mr Everton headed for some seats in the bay window overlooking the inn's garden. "Come on, kids, we'll sit by the window."

Candy and Jake followed him, but as they sat down Candy couldn't help noticing the puzzled look on his face.

"What are you thinking, Dad?" she whispered as they sat down.

"I'm thinking someone's got a guilty conscience regarding this brandy," he murmured. "Don't know why they got so uptight. I wasn't suggesting it was bootleg or anything."

"What's bootleg?" Jake asked.

"It means it's been imported and sold on without paying this country's tax on it," his dad explained.

Candy glanced at the inn keepers. The runner had joined them now and they were all talking quietly. They definitely looked as if they were up to something.

"Actually," whispered Candy, "it wouldn't surprise me if they were all involved in something illegal. Just look at them huddled together."

"Yeah!" hissed Jake, his eyes lighting up. "Remember what that landlady said – Benjamin never cheated them, and he was fair. Perhaps Benjamin was a smuggler, smuggling bootleg brandy into the country."

Candy laughed. "Jake, I don't think you could sail a narrowboat across the English Channel without being noticed."

"No, but you could go across in a lorry," Jake whispered, glancing furtively at the runner. "He said he was a long-distance lorry driver on the Continent. Maybe he brings bootleg brandy from abroad. Maybe he used to pass it to Benjamin and he cruised up the canal selling all the smuggled stuff to the pubs on the way."

"Whoa!" their dad stopped them. "Kids, I'm all for an active imagination, but don't let's get carried away. We've enough drama on our hands without making matters worse."

"But Dad," Candy argued, "Jake could be right."

Their discussion went on for the next half-hour or so and only came to a halt when two police officers walked into the inn. The younger one was in uniform, tall and thin, with a fresh, cheery face. The other was in plain clothes, but quite obviously a policeman by the way his sharp eyes swept over them all.

Everyone instantly sat to attention, except the fisherman who almost knocked his drink flying.

"Steady on, sir," said the younger officer, stopping the glass from skidding off the table.

The plain-clothes detective raised one eyebrow as he looked down at the nervous fisherman. "Oh hello, sir. It's Mr Rathbone, isn't it?"

"Yes," the little man gulped, almost choking on the word. "I'm surprised you remembered me, Inspector Meade."

"Never forget a case, Mr Rathbone, particularly unsolved ones," the Inspector replied. "Odd, isn't it, sir? More than a year's gone by and still not one piece of the stolen goods has ever come to light."

"Yes, it's most baffling," the fisherman agreed, fiddling with his glass.

Inspector Meade continued looking at the nervous little fisherman for a moment, and then smiled. "We haven't given up yet though, sir. Anyway, how are you enjoying your retirement?"

"Oh, it's fine, thank you. Bit of fishing, bit of gardening—"

"Still doing the martial arts?"

"Oh yes," the fisherman said with the hint of a nervous smile.

Candy's eyebrows shot up. Martial arts! She couldn't think of anyone less likely. He looked so puny.

"Knew the deceased, did you, Mr Rathbone?" Inspector Meade continued, chatting amicably to the fisherman.

The fisherman seemed nervous at all this attention and gripped his glass with both hands, as if trying to stop it, or himself, from shaking. "We passed the time of day," he gulped nervously.

The Inspector nodded and then addressed everyone in the pub. "My man will need to take statements from you all. It shouldn't take too long. Your co-operation will be appreciated."

"Inspector," the landlady interrupted, holding her handkerchief to her mouth again, "how did poor Benjamin die?"

"Drowning I'd say, madam. There'll have to be an autopsy before we can be certain, but I imagine the poor old soul slipped and fell overboard."

"Drunk!" the postwoman said loudly.

The Inspector wandered over to her. "Partial to a drink, was he, Miss. . .?"

"Ellis. Kitty Ellis," the postwoman answered stiffly. "And yes, he most certainly did like his drink. He had bottles of the stuff!"

Behind the bar, Candy noticed the landlord removing the bottle of brandy from his shelf and slipping it under the counter out of sight.

"Did he indeed?" said the Inspector, looking around again. "So who actually discovered the body?"

"My daughter did," Mr Everton spoke up. "We're the new owners of the *Baloo*. We're spending the weekend sprucing her up a bit. It's been a bit of a shock."

"I can well imagine," Inspector Meade acknowledged. "My men are going over the boat now. I hate to ask, but would you and your children accompany me back to the boat so I can get a clear understanding of how the body reappeared?"

Candy stared in horror at her dad. Immediately the Inspector calmed her unspoken fears.

"Don't worry. My men have already removed

the body. I just want to go over the events lead-
ing up to you discovering it."

"Oh, right. OK then," Candy agreed, getting
up.

"We'll probably put a frogman down just to
make sure there's no one else down there or
anything peculiar," commented the Inspector
as he headed for the door. "Although everything points to a tragic accident. I've no reason
at this stage to think there was foul play. Folk
around here live pretty simple, uncomplicated
lives."

Candy glanced back at the others in the pub.
The runner and the inn keepers were silent
now, but still communicating with nervous,
shifty glances. The fisherman was sweating.
The postwoman, Kitty Ellis, was clearly
delighted Benjamin was dead. And as for the
lock-keeper, Ted Johnstone, he had looked
positively relieved at the turn of events.

Simple and uncomplicated? She didn't think
so.

5

Candy had never seen so many policemen. They were swarming all over the *Baloo* – down in the cabin, up on the deck, on the towpath, everywhere.

"So you're renovating the boat, Mr Everton?" Inspector Meade asked, trying to put him at ease as they walked along the towpath towards the *Baloo*.

Her dad looked as shocked as Candy felt on seeing so many policemen all over their boat, but he answered as brightly as he could. "Yes, I've actually been after the *Baloo* for years. First spotted her a few years back in a marina on a canal-side open day." He smiled wistfully. "I've always had a yen for narrowboats and canals and stuff. I suppose owning a boat has been my ultimate dream."

"Well, let's hope this hasn't become a nightmare for you, sir," said the Inspector as they reached the *Baloo*.

For the next half-hour or so, Candy, Jake and their dad went over the whole series of events for the police, explaining how another boat had sped past and caused their boat to rock so badly it had dislodged poor Benjamin Fisher's body.

As they talked and answered question after question, another officer took photographs of everything – the boat, the water, and them. Candy was feeling quite exhausted by the time the police had finished.

Inspector Meade finally looked satisfied. "Sorry to put you through this, but we have to get all the facts straight. It does seem like the poor man slipped and fell overboard. It all goes to show, kids, you can't be too careful where water is concerned. Always wear your life jackets."

"We will," Jake promised.

As all the policemen left the *Baloo*, Inspector Meade turned back to Mr Everton. "We'll probably send a frogman down tomorrow or the day after. Just routine. We'll try not to be too intrusive. Thanks for all your help."

As the last officer disappeared along the towpath back to the main road, Mr Everton heaved a sigh of relief. "I need a cup of tea after that. The flask's below decks. Come on."

They went down into the galley. Everything was just as they had left it, although the police had probably examined every cupboard. Mr Everton poured tea from his flask and they sat at the bench table feeling totally exhausted.

"We'd better phone your mum and tell her what's happened," Mr Everton decided. "Finish your tea and we'll take a walk back to the main road. There's a phone box there."

"You could ring from the pub," Jake suggested.

Mr Everton wrinkled his nose. "No, I reckon a walk will do us good. Clear our heads. Come on, let's go."

The walk back to the main road took ten minutes or so. Mrs Everton was horrified to hear what they had discovered. She ordered them all home immediately, and took some convincing that everything really was all right.

When they had finally talked her around, they wandered slowly back to the *Baloo*. Mr Everton looked weary.

"What shall we do, kids – call it a day? I don't think we're really in the mood for doing anything now, are we?"

"I don't mind," Jake said enthusiastically.

A glimmer of hope registered on his dad's face. Candy knew this was the only long weekend he had free to work on the boat. And he had been so looking forward to getting it cleaned up. But still, she felt slightly uneasy at the thought of sorting through Benjamin's belongings now that she knew he was dead. Still, if Jake could handle it, so could she.

"I don't mind either, Dad," she said, hooking her arm through his.

"Are you sure?" Mr Everton asked, brightening.

"Absolutely!" smiled Candy.

"OK. That's great. Right, let's carry on where we left off. I'll have another go at the engine, and you two get tidying below decks."

As they reached the *Baloo*, he jumped on board and eagerly lifted the engine compartment lid. Then, getting down on hands and knees, he poked his head into the oily compartment.

"My, that looks fun," Candy said wryly, leaving her dad to tinker with the engine as she led the way down into the galley.

But the sight that met her and Jake stopped them dead in their tracks.

The place had been ransacked. Every drawer had been upturned, the contents of every cupboard pulled out. Papers, clothes, crockery and gadgets were scattered all over the place.

"Oh Jake!" Candy breathed. "What a mess! Why would anyone do this? Why?"

"They must have been searching for something," said Jake quietly.

"The brandy!" Candy exclaimed, diving down to the cupboard where it had been stored. It was still there.

She shook her head, baffled. "Not the brandy. . . What then? And why would anyone break in now? The *Baloo*'s been standing empty for over a year. Why ransack it today?"

"Beats me," murmured Jake.

"Unless . . ." breathed Candy, her eyes widening . . . "unless they were after something they didn't know *existed* until today."

"Like what?"

Her eyes were huge. "Like Benjamin Fisher's diary!"

Jake's mouth dropped open. "Hey, right! Remember the way they all stared at me when I told them Benjamin kept a diary? Like they were all desperate to get their hands on it?"

Candy's face dropped as she looked around at the mess and clutter. "And now it looks like someone has."

"Not quite," said Jake as a slow grin crept over his face.

"What do you mean?"

Slowly he reached into the back pocket of his jeans – and pulled out the crumpled notebook.

Benjamin Fisher's secret diary!

6

Almost afraid to breathe, Candy opened Benjamin's diary. It was simply a fat school exercise book, but Benjamin had logged something down faithfully every day from January 1st to June 22nd of the previous year.

"That's the last entry – June 22nd," Candy murmured, feeling incredibly sad suddenly. Was that the day Benjamin Fisher had died?

"What does it say? Go on, read it," Jake urged, hanging over her shoulder.

Candy hesitated. It didn't seem right – reading someone's private thoughts. "Oh, I don't know. . ."

"You've got to. It might be important," Jake pestered.

Candy chewed nervously on her lip. Jake was right – it might be important. In fact someone thought it important enough to make all this mess trying to find it.

Taking a deep breath, she flipped back the pages to the beginning of the year. Guiltily she looked down at the flamboyant handwriting.

"Read it aloud, Candy," Jake begged.

"Oh, all right. Now, let's see. January 1st, 9pm. . .

Wasted day. Canal's frozen for miles. Still stuck here, loaded to the hilt. Hope I don't get any 'visitors'. Weather men say a thaw is on the way. Don't look like it to me. Snowing heavily all day."

"Loaded to the hilt?" Jake repeated. "With bootleg brandy, I bet. And by 'visitors', I expect he means the police."

Candy turned a couple of pages. For most of January Benjamin was complaining about the weather. Ice seemed to be slowing him down. "Here's something, Jake," she read. "January 19th. . .

Made good progress today. Eighteen miles and five drops. Should reach Oxford by the end of the week."

"Five drops!" said Jake excitedly. "He's dropping off the brandy."

"You don't know that, Jake."

"I bet he is. Anyway, go on, read some more."

Candy flicked through a few more pages. Judging by the place names mentioned in Benjamin's diary, he was travelling north. "He certainly gets about. I thought boat people lived lazy kind of lives. Benjamin seems to have travelled miles every day."

"That's because he's running a business – funny business!" Jake grinned. Then his smile dropped. "Or rather he *was* running a business."

"March 12th, 9.30pm," Candy read.

"Bilge pump started playing up again. Got me a nice friendly welcome from them at the Anchor. Had me a nice piece of steak. Free – well, it would be, wouldn't it?"

"Skip a bit," Jake suggested, starting to fidget.

Candy sighed. "You know, I really hate doing this. It's private."

"He's not going to know," Jake reminded her.

"No. I suppose not," Candy agreed, turning a few pages.

"June 1st, 10pm. Reached Leadbury at noon. Bumped into Kitty Ellis delivering the midday post. Can't say she was pleased to see me. Where a lady learns such language beats me. I mean, it weren't me who was too idle to deliver them letters. So why's she got to take it out on me?

Had a bit of fun winding her up. Told her I was still thinking about reporting her. Lord, does that woman rise to the bait! Still, it's worth being on the receiving end of her tongue to get my apple pies. No one makes apple pies like Kitty!"

Candy glanced at her brother. "I don't think he was going to report her at all. I think he enjoyed teasing her. And it looks like she gave him apple pies to keep him quiet."

"Well, she wouldn't have pushed him overboard," said Jake, grinning. "She'd just have poisoned his pudding!"

Candy closed the diary and glanced around the galley. "We'd better get this mess cleared up. If Dad sees this lot, he'll have a fit."

"But we didn't do it," Jake reminded her.

"I know, but we still ought to tidy it up."

"Read a bit more first," urged Jake.

Candy smoothed the dog-eared pages of the old notebook, wondering if someone really had broken in to try and find Benjamin's diary. Was it that important?

She read on.

"June 5th, 9.45pm. Staying in Leadbury for a few days. That don't please Ted much."

"Ted? Who's Ted?" Jake asked.

"Could be Ted Johnstone, the lock-keeper," suggested Candy, reading on.

"Think I made him nervous. Ain't life grand! He'll be glad when he gets his 50 years' long service medal. He'll be able to relax and retire then. 50 years of unblemished service to the waterways. Good old Ted! Well, if he don't tell them, I won't. Shan't tell him that though. Keeps him on his toes – and off my back!

The old goat was a mischief-maker!" Candy exclaimed. "He seems to have known everyone's guilty secret!"

"Wonder what guilty secret the lock-keeper had, then?" Jake said, puzzled. "Anyway, read some more, Candy – nearer to his last days."

Eagerly Candy turned the pages.

"June 19th, 7pm. It was all over the newspapers. Well, who'd have believed it! Now this will ruffle a few feathers. Could earn me a pound or two if I just let slip that I know all about it. . ."

Candy stared at her brother. "Jake, I think Benjamin Fisher was a bit of a blackmailer. Pies from the postwoman. The lock-keeper keeping off his back – whatever that means. Now he's discovered something which might earn him some money. Oh Jake. . ."

Jake's eyes widened. "You don't think that someone got fed up with him blackmailing them, and got rid of him, do you?"

Candy bit her lip. "I think that's quite likely."

Jake inched closer. "Keep reading."

"June 20th, 8.30pm. Spent the day painting. Nice

little picture. A picture paints a thousand words! Dropped a subtle hint. Beats me why people do these naughty little crimes if they don't like being found out.

June 21st, 11pm. Had a good meal at the King Edward today. What kind hosts we have there! Wouldn't accept a penny off me! Oh happy days!"

Jake pulled a face. "He *was* a blackmailer. No doubt about it. Go on, Candy – see if June 22nd, his last day, gives us any more clues."

Candy sighed. "I should think if he was getting all his food free, he got lots of beer free too. Probably the postwoman was right: he was drunk and fell overboard."

"Just read, will you!"

"OK, OK. . .

June 22nd, 12 midnight. Should have kept my mouth shut. Sensed it tonight. I've gone too far. Got to get away quick, while I still can. I'm so stupid. Should have left well alone. Been jumpy all day. Scared. Me scared! Never been scared before. Keep hearing things. Bumps, noises, footsteps. Can hear something now – footsteps up on deck. It's my imagination, I know. I'll have to double-check though. Then I'll leave at first light. Leadbury Junction – you can keep it."

Candy turned the page. It was blank. So was the next page and the next. That was the last thing Benjamin Fisher had ever written.

7

"He was murdered!"

"You can't be certain of that, Jake," Candy argued.

"But I *am* certain. In fact I'm positive!" Jake hissed, trying to keep his voice down. "Benjamin Fisher was a second-rate black-mailer. Only he blackmailed the wrong person and they didn't like it."

Candy had to admit, it did seem like that. She glanced back through the diary to June 19th. "It must be connected with the crime he read about in the newspaper."

"Yeah, maybe he knew who did it," agreed Jake.

Candy wrinkled her nose. "If only we knew what crime he was talking about, or who was involved. . ."

Jake's eyes became huge – frightened almost. "Candy, it might be the same person who ransacked the *Baloo* looking for the diary."

She stared at her brother. The thought that a murderer might have just been in here made her shudder. "Not necessarily, because *everyone* looked like they'd kill to get their hands on it. And they can't all be murderers, can they?"

Jake pulled an evil face. "Leadbury Junction – murderers' paradise. Enter at your peril!"

"Shut up, Jake," Candy groaned. "Anyway, we'd better get this mess cleared up. Only. . ."

"Only what?"

She chewed on her lip thoughtfully. "Watch what you're throwing away. There might be a clue or something."

Jake's eyes lit up. "What sort of a clue?"

"I don't know," Candy exclaimed. "Just keep your eyes open."

Bit by bit, they either threw away Benjamin's old possessions, or put them back tidily in the cupboards. Mostly it was junk. But they kept all his letters in case they provided a clue, and pots of paint that weren't dried up, and his tools.

Jake was just about to screw a newspaper up to throw it away when Candy grabbed his arm.

"Hang on! Benjamin said it was all over the newspapers – the crime thing. What's the date on that paper?"

Jake smoothed out the front page, then let out a great whoop of delight. "Hey! June 19th last year! That's the date he said. Oh, wow! This will give us the answer. This is gonna tell us who murdered Benjamin Fisher!"

Candy frowned. "Jake, we don't know it was murder."

He pulled a face. "I bet it was. Something scared Benjamin. He was ready to leave Leadbury Junction before they got him. Then he heard footsteps up on deck, went to investigate, and was never seen again. Well, not till today."

Candy spread the newspaper out over the table. She wasn't sure what she was looking for. It was a pity Benjamin hadn't circled the article with a red pen.

Still, she didn't have to look far for a crime. It was the local newspaper and the front page headline screamed of a raid on the town's jewellery shop.

Eagerly she read how despite the owner's attempts to fight off two burly masked raiders by using his martial arts skills, he was no match for them. They had got away with a quarter of a million pounds' worth of jewellery.

Candy read and re-read the article. The owner had been alone and about to close up for the night when the masked raiders burst in. The shop owner, Mr Arthur Rathbone, was being hailed a hero for putting up a tremendous battle. He told reporters that although he was fully insured for theft, the trauma of the attack made him feel like getting out of the jewellery business for good.

"Rathbone?" Candy murmured. That name rang a bell, didn't it? She just couldn't think why, though.

And two burly masked raiders? Perhaps Benjamin knew who they were.

With a sigh, she turned the pages. There were pictures from the local town carnival, with everyone having fun. News of jumble sales and school fairs. Two or three burglaries. A whole page of wedding photographs. . .

One photograph caught her eye. It was the landlord and landlady of *The King Edward Inn* getting married!

Candy's eyes widened. She had assumed they had been married for years. Obviously not.

She read their names: Kieran and Katherine Elizabeth Eastwood. Not much to blackmail anyone about there, was there?

Turning the pages until she reached the motoring section, another photograph stared out at her. For a second Candy couldn't think where she knew him from. Then she remembered.

It was the runner. His name was Jason Quinn and he had just won the Lorry Driver of the Year Competition.

"So what do you reckon?" Jake asked.

Candy sighed. "Well, Benjamin wrote that it was all over the newspapers. And *it* was something worth blackmailing someone over. It has to be the jewellery theft. It just has to be!"

"Perhaps he discovered who the robbers were," Jake suggested excitedly.

"Two burly masked raiders," Candy said,

mainly to herself. "Who do we know who's burly?"

Jake thought for a moment. "Ted Johnstone the lock-keeper?"

"Yes," Candy agreed. "And the landlord of *The King Edward Inn*. He's pretty burly."

"So's his wife," grinned Jake.

With a groan Candy flopped back in her seat and stared through the little cabin window at the rippling water. There was a duck paddling alongside and she watched it, lost in thought.

Jake got up and stretched. "Well, while you're thinking down here, I'm going to have a think out in the sunshine."

Candy didn't bother answering. She was too busy trying to work out what exactly Benjamin had seen in the newspaper that cost him his life.

Maybe it wasn't murder at all. Maybe she was being stupid listening to Jake. These were respectable people. They weren't murderers. Benjamin probably did just fall overboard.

Eventually, she gave up and went out into the sunlight. Her dad was sitting on the bench seat by the tiller, eating a pork pie.

"You've emerged then. Hungry?"

She wrinkled her nose. "Not really. Where's Jake?"

"Up front," her dad replied, adding, "We'll have a nice meal at the Inn later. We've hardly eaten a thing all day."

"OK," Candy smiled, walking carefully along the gunnel to the bow.

Jake was stretched out on the bow, half asleep. He opened one eye as she perched herself next to him. "Discover anything?"

She shook her head. "Not really. I don't think he was murdered at all. He probably just fell overboard."

Jake rolled on to his stomach and peered down to where Benjamin had been found. He was silent for a minute, then said, "If I fell in, I'd just haul myself out again on these ropes. Or I'd swim to the bank. . . Hang on, what's this?"

He stretched further over the bow, till his head was almost in the water. Automatically Candy grabbed his ankles.

"Jake, canal water does not make good shampoo!"

"I'm looking at something," he muttered.

"What? Jake, what is it?"

"Scratches – scratches in the paintwork.

They're all rusty now, but it looks as if someone has scratched some letters. Hang on, they're upside down and back to front."

Still hanging on to her brother, Candy leant over too. She saw the scratches immediately.

And from the angle they were written, they could only have been written by somebody in the water. . .

A shiver ran down her spine. Had Benjamin made these scratches? Had someone pushed him in and held him underwater? Her eyes flew to the bargepole. Had they used that to hold him down?

Unable to reach dry land or haul himself out, had Benjamin realized he was drowning and done the only thing he could? Tried to write his killer's name?

"See them, Candy?" Jake gasped. "See them?"

"Yes, I see them. There's a K and an E." She hauled her brother upright, her expression grave. "Jake, I think we'd better tell the police. Benjamin Fisher was definitely murdered – and the killer's initials are KE!"

8

"No!" Mr Everton said sternly. "No, we are not going to the police with some ridiculous fairy tale. For one thing, you've no proof. Secondly, you'll get decent people involved. And thirdly, we've only just got rid of the police. The last thing we want is them swarming all over the *Baloo* again."

"But Dad—"

"No buts, Candy. Now, I suggest you both put this nonsense out of your heads. You'll be giving yourselves nightmares." He heaved a sigh then and smiled kindly. "Look, how about taking a break? Grab a sandwich, both of you, and we'll go for a walk along to the locks. We can watch the boats going through – it won't be long before we'll have to work them ourselves."

"OK," Candy murmured, disappointed that her dad didn't realize the importance of their discovery. "Come on, Jake. . ." she lowered her voice, ". . .and bring the diary."

Locking the cabin door, they set off along the towpath towards the locks and the big iron bridge. The lock-keeper's cottage was a tiny stone building with a door that scarcely looked big enough for Ted Johnstone to get through.

They went up on to the iron bridge that spanned the canal. At the top Candy leant on the cold girder and gazed down at the lock-keeper's cottage.

What had Benjamin written about him? Something about fifty years of perfect service to the waterways. Then he'd hinted that it hadn't been all perfect. Obviously Benjamin knew something – some guilty secret.

Candy couldn't help wondering whether the lock-keeper had pushed Benjamin overboard and held him under. Had he made sure that Benjamin would never give away his guilty secret?

Candy groaned to herself. If that was the case, why hadn't Benjamin written Ted, or TJ instead of KE?

The hairs at the back of her neck began to prickle. Unless . . . he was trying to write *KE – KEEPER. Lock-keeper!*

"Jake!"

"Shush! I was just trying to work something out."

"Kids, I'm just going to look at that boat over there," interrupted Mr Everton as he strode off over the bridge. "She's a beauty!"

"Jake!" Candy said urgently. "Jake, those letters, KE. Benjamin might have been trying to write KEEPER – lock-keeper."

Jake screwed up his face. "I dunno. I was thinking that KE might stand for *The King Edward Inn*."

Candy chewed her lip. "Possibly – or the landlord and landlady. Kieran and Katherine Elizabeth Eastwood – KE and KEE."

Jake's eyebrows rose. "Wish we knew what that runner's name was. He's in cahoots with them. You could tell by their whispering."

Candy tried to remember what the newspaper had written about him. Lorry Driver of the Year. "Jason something. That's it – Jason Quinn. JQ. He's out then."

"Who else wanted Benjamin out of the way?" Candy wondered. "Oh yes, the postwoman, Kitty Ellis. Oh help! Everyone has the initials KE."

"You're not kidding!" Jake gasped, his eyes wide. "I've just thought of someone else."

"Who? The fisherman? We don't know his name . . . do we?" Candy said, feeling as if she ought to know it.

"No, not him," Jake said, peering over the bridge at their dad fussing around a moored narrowboat. "What's *our* surname?"

"Everton," Candy murmured, knowing what he was about to say.

"And Dad's first name?"

"Jake, don't be so stupid. That's our dad you're talking about."

"I know. But you can't deny it: Dad's name is Kevin. Kevin Everton. KE! And he always wanted to own the *Baloo* – Benjamin Fisher's boat."

"Jake, you say some really stupid things sometimes," Candy snapped angrily, giving her brother a shove before running down to join her dad on the towpath. "Really stupid."

Jake followed her down, but as they stood silently by their dad at the water's edge they were joined by Ted Johnstone.

Suddenly Candy felt cold. She linked her arm through her dad's.

"Police gone and left you in peace then?" the lock-keeper asked, staring at Candy and Jake with hard, steely blue eyes.

"Yes, thank goodness," Mr Everton replied. "Bit of a shock, that was."

"Indeed, indeed," agreed the lock-keeper, stroking his grey speckled beard.

"Had you known Benjamin Fisher long?" Mr Everton asked.

Ted gazed off into the distance as he replied. "Oh yes, a long, long time. We've both had a lifetime on the canals."

"What was he like?" Candy asked, hoping she didn't look as uneasy as she felt.

"Ben?" the lock-keeper said, staring off into the distance. "Let's say that he was a bit of a rogue. He lived off his wits. He'd take advantage of a situation. He'd see something that didn't concern him, and turn it round so that it benefited him in some way. A crafty old dog was Benjamin Fisher."

Candy wanted to know more. She wanted to ask the lock-keeper what *his* secret was. Something about him not having a spotless record of service. Something that had happened and which he wasn't proud of.

Benjamin knew what it was. And the lock-keeper knew that Benjamin knew. It kept him off Benjamin's back.

So if, for example, Benjamin was smuggling illegal stuff from the Continent, the lock-keeper didn't ask questions because he knew Benjamin could tell tales on him too.

Their attention switched to another narrow-boat cruising slowly into the lock. A boy of about Candy's age jumped off to close the massive lock gates behind the boat.

As the boat glided into the lock, the boy expertly wound the paddle down behind it to close the lock gates. Then, running ahead, he flipped open the other paddle to allow the lock to flood.

Candy watched fascinated as foaming canal water flushed through the lock gates and the narrowboat slowly rose higher and higher.

"I'll never get the hang of that," Candy murmured, watching as the boy began to cross the tiny bridge formed by the lock gates. Suddenly his foot slipped and he stumbled.

The lock-keeper moved swiftly. In seconds he was on the little bridge and had grabbed the boy to steady him.

"Careful, lad!"

The boy pulled a face and grinned, embarrassed that he'd nearly fallen into the lock with everyone watching him. "It's OK, I can swim," he boasted.

Holding on to the boy's arm until the narrowboat was level and he could get back on board, the lock-keeper gave him and his family a lecture on canal safety.

When finally he let them go on their way, he strode back to Candy and Jake. Candy thought how pale he looked.

"Showing off! Silly little kid," he grumbled, "telling me he can swim! You can't swim with tonnes of water crashing down on your head and barely fifteen centimetres spare between you, a ten-tonne narrowboat and brick walls."

Mr Everton agreed. "Quite right. There's no fooling around near water. I'm always telling these two."

"We don't fool about!" Jake protested.

"Lucky for him I was here," Ted Johnstone continued, still looking ashen. As he ran his fingers through his grey hair, Candy saw that his hands were trembling. "You can't always be there, can you?" he went on, almost talking to himself. "We haven't eyes in the back of our heads. Someone drowns and who gets the blame? Me! My fault. It's my locks. I'm in charge. So it's me to blame!"

Candy stared at him. He was getting into quite a state.

Her dad seemed to be of the same opinion. "Did the police question you about Benjamin Fisher too?" he asked sympathetically.

The lock-keeper frowned, as if he'd forgotten all about Benjamin Fisher. "No. Why should they? Benjamin didn't drown in my lock. Nothing to do with me. I'm not taking the blame. Oh no. No, siree. That's not my business at all."

"No one is suggesting it was," said Mr Everton, trying to calm the older man down. "He probably just fell overboard. A tragic accident."

The lock-keeper said nothing, but stood there, his chest going up and down as if trying to control his emotions.

In an effort to change the subject Mr Everton said casually, "How long have you worked the locks then, Mr Johnstone?"

"He's been here fifty years," Jake piped up.

The lock-keeper shot him a startled look, then narrowed his eyes. "How do you know that, boy? Someone been talking about me?"

"Er . . . no, I just heard," Jake muttered, his hand going automatically to his back pocket and the diary.

The lock-keeper's eyes followed him. He looked as if he didn't believe Jake. He looked as if he knew the diary was there. He looked as if he believed that Candy and Jake knew his secret.

But then he relaxed. Puffing his chest out, he said, "Well, m'lad, you're absolutely right. Next month I'll be celebrating fifty years working these locks, man and boy. Learnt everything from my father, and his father before that. We've a long tradition of keeping these locks in the Johnstone family." He actually smiled. "Think I'm due for a little presentation. There'll be a bit of a do. Town Mayor's coming, and the newspapers."

"Do many people get drowned on the waterways?" Candy asked impulsively, guessing she was stirring things up. But with her arm through her dad's, there was nothing to be afraid of.

The lock-keeper shook his head slowly. "Leadbury Junction has an impeccable record, I'm proud to say."

"You mean there's never been any accidents here?" Candy went on, wishing he would give something away about the secret only he and Benjamin knew.

She suddenly had the feeling that she was getting close.

The lock-keeper's small eyes flinched. He looked quizzically at her, so that even with her dad beside her, the hairs at the back of her neck began to prickle.

"Have you *heard* something?" he asked menacingly.

"No!" Candy said defensively. "Why? Is there something to hear?"

He looked decidedly angry, but Candy stood her ground, unflinching. It was her dad who was embarrassed. Jovially he said, "Right, kids, time to get back to work. Lots still to be done. Nice talking to you, Mr Johnstone."

The lock-keeper nodded. "Aye, interesting

talking to you three as well. I'll be seeing you."

They walked away, but still Candy could feel the man's hard, questioning eyes boring into the back of her head.

Murderous eyes, she had thought. Maybe because they *were* the eyes of a murderer.

9

Candy was glad to get back to the *Baloo*. Once on board, her dad gave her a stern look. "I assume that little interrogation has something to do with your fanciful notion about a murderer on the loose."

"I wish you'd believe us!" Candy exclaimed, as she perched herself by the tiller. "We reckon someone murdered Benjamin because he knew too much."

"About what?" her dad asked, folding his arms and looking vaguely amused.

"You heard what Ted Johnstone said, Dad," Jake argued. "Benjamin was an old rogue. He nosed about and got to know people's secrets. And we think he was a smuggler."

"Not again!" Mr Everton groaned. "Honestly, you two, you make me laugh, you really do. Kids, this isn't a pirate ship. We're not sailing down to the caves and the coves of old Cornwall in the seventeenth century."

Jake glared indignantly. "He's a modern-day smuggler. The runner drives a lorry on the Continent. He buys that brandy and probably other stuff by the tonne. Benjamin meets him somewhere and takes the booze off him."

Candy took over the story. "Then he cruises up the canals, selling it at a profit to all the pubs on the way."

Still grinning as he unlocked the galley door, Mr Everton added, "And he cheated someone so they made him walk the plank."

"In a way, yes," Jake agreed, following him below deck.

Candy thought back to what the pub landlady had said: *Benjamin was a good man, he never cheated us. . .*

"It wasn't the landlady," she said, going below after them. "He never cheated them."

"No, I don't think it was her either," agreed

Jake. "She's the only one who's really upset that he's dead. So how many more KE's have we got to eliminate, Candy?"

Mr Everton shook his head in despair. "So the murderer has the initials KE? Well, you'd better add me to your list."

"We already have," Jake announced, then looked guilty as his dad's face dropped. "Oh, don't worry, we know you didn't do it."

"Well, thank you!" he exclaimed.

Candy gave him a hug. "Ignore him. He can be really stupid sometimes. Let's stick with the real suspects, shall we Jake?"

Her dad sat down at the table and pushed the red painted kettle to one side. "Here's another idea for you kids."

"What?" they asked eagerly.

"Pub landlady's surname begins with an E according to you."

"Yes, it's Eastwood," said Candy.

"So her husband's Eastwood too – and I over-heard in the pub someone calling him Kieran. So he's one of your suspects too."

"Yes," Candy said, puzzled, wondering what he was getting at.

"She was *very* upset," said their dad pointedly.

"And?" Candy urged.

He wiggled his eyebrows. "Perhaps there was some romantic connection between her and Benjamin. Maybe her husband got jealous and pushed him overboard."

Candy thought for a minute, then pulled a face. "I don't know. According to Benjamin's diary it's connected with something that was in the newspaper on June 19th. A crime of some sort. It might be to do with a jewellery raid."

Jake grabbed her arm. "Their wedding photo was in the paper. Dad, you could be right. Maybe the pub landlord did do it – in a fit of jealous rage. Wow!"

"Who knows?" Mr Everton shrugged, digging into his pocket for some cash. "But you can mull it over while you're fetching some ice-creams. That little shop's still open by the looks of it."

The shop was sandwiched between *The King Edward Inn* and the postwoman's cottage. The door made a tinkling, chiming sound as Candy and Jake went in.

An old woman with straggly grey hair smiled toothlessly from behind the counter. She was sucking a sweet while her husband, equally as grey and toothless, was polishing a horse-brass.

Candy and Jake delved among the sparse contents of the fridge and emerged with two ice lollies. Candy just hoped they weren't past their sell-by date. She decided not to check but paid the money and made to leave.

"They found him then?" the old woman clucked.

Candy turned sharply. "Sorry?"

The old woman's sunken eyes were bright. "Benjamin. We saw the commotion this morning. Police came and talked to us. So that's two then."

Candy stared at her. "Two? Two what?"

Either she hadn't heard or she didn't care to answer Candy directly. Turning to her husband, she said, "Two, isn't it, Henry? Two people that have drowned here at Leadbury."

The old man didn't look up. Instead he spat on the horse-brass and polished harder, as if he would rub the pattern off. "Aye, two now."

"Two?" Candy echoed, glancing at her brother. "Who's the other one then?"

The old woman manoeuvred her sweet into her cheek, so that it stuck out like a boil. "A kiddie. Boy, I think. Henry, it were a boy, weren't it? A little lad?"

He nodded.

The old woman swivelled her tiny sunken bright eyes back to Candy. "Aye, a little lad."

"When did this happen? How . . . who. . .?"

"Oh, a long, long time ago. Years and years. Most folk round here are too young to remember."

"What happened?" Jake pestered, practically leaning over the counter to catch her quietly spoken voice.

She blew her nose before answering. "Kiddie was just playing, like kiddies do. Messing about with the locks. Didn't see the danger. Poor little lamb."

Candy's forehead furrowed. "But when we spoke to the lock-keeper he said no one had ever drowned here at Leadbury."

For once the old man glanced up from his work. He cast a watery look at his wife, then at Candy and Jake. In a crackly old voice he said, "Aye, well, he would say that, wouldn't he?"

10

Whether the ice lollies were past their sell-by date or not, they tasted good. Candy and Jake strolled along the towpath, deep in discussion about what the old couple had told them.

"Do you reckon *that's* the lock-keeper's dark secret?" Jake wondered.

"It might be," Candy agreed. "Benjamin wrote something about fifty years' perfect service. Someone drowning would spoil his perfect record a bit, wouldn't it?"

"But it happened years ago," Jake reminded her.

"All the more reason why he doesn't want it

brought up now," said Candy. "He's about to be presented with his fifty-year-long service medal or something."

Jake wiped a trickle of orange juice from his chin. "Yeah, but would he kill just for that?"

"Mmm, it is a bit drastic," Candy agreed. "And why stop there? That old couple knew too."

Jake thought for a minute, then, "Ah, but what if Benjamin *threatened* to tell everyone?"

Candy stared at her little brother. He wasn't stupid all the time, after all. "Jake, you've got a point there. That lock-keeper has a high opinion of himself. I don't think he could stand the shame of not being perfect." She clutched his arm. "Jake . . . I think he could be the murderer."

Jake's eyes widened. "Yeah, remember how he just stared and stared at Benjamin's body in the water? Like he was remembering. . ."

"And that look on his face. . ."

"Hello, you two. Enjoying your ice lollies?"

They were so engrossed in conversation, they hadn't noticed the fisherman still sitting there, fishing.

"Oh! Hello again," Candy smiled, wondering

how anybody could fish in a canal where a dead body had just been dragged out.

He was sitting on a little fold-up chair, surrounded by an array of tackle and bait. Jake immediately crouched down beside him. "What are you after?"

The fisherman cast him a strange look, then, grasping what Jake was talking about, said, "Oh! Er . . . perch, gudgeon. You'd be surprised what you can catch here." He smiled and a gold tooth caught the sun and dazzled them.

He wasn't joking, Candy thought. It wasn't everywhere you could hook a dead body.

While Jake and the fisherman discussed fishing techniques, Candy glanced at all his bits and pieces. She was glad there weren't any maggots. Fishermen always seemed to have a bowl of maggots. She'd heard a story once about how they warmed maggots up by putting them in their mouths first to make them wriggle more.

Feeling her stomach churn, she glanced down at pleasanter things. He had a nice wicker basket, like an old-fashioned picnic hamper. It had a little leather tag on it with initials etched in goldleaf – AR. She was glad they weren't KE.

Then something else caught her eye: a large grey weight with a metal loop at the top. "What's this?" she asked.

"Don't touch anything now, children," the fisherman fretted, swivelling round in his chair to see what she was examining. Jake stretched over and took it off her.

"It's a magnet. Wow! I've never seen one this big. What's it for?"

The fisherman's moustache twitched. The gold tooth glinted. "I once dropped my car keys into the canal. Got them out with a magnet. I keep it with me, just in case."

"Good idea," said Jake. "We've got our boat key fastened to a chunk of wood, so it'll float if we drop it overboard."

Talking about things falling into the canal seemed to make the fisherman nervous again. He rubbed his gold-ringed hand over his trousers, as if his palm was clammy. "Bad do, that. Poor Benjamin. Police have gone now, I see. Will they be back for more statements and things?"

Jake shrugged. "Dunno. Oh yeah, a frogman is coming tomorrow or the day after."

"So they are sending one. I wondered if they

would," the fisherman murmured, speaking almost to himself. "Tomorrow or Monday, you say?"

"I think so," Candy replied.

"You don't know when exactly?"

"No, sorry," she said, frowning and wondering if he was planning to come and watch.

"Hey, mister," Jake suddenly exclaimed. "You've got a bite!"

"What? Oh yes, so I have," he murmured vaguely, staring at the tight line as if he hadn't a clue what to do now.

"Reel it in then!" Jake yelled.

"Right!" he said, taking the rod in both hands and reeling his catch in. A large silvery wriggling fish suddenly rose out of the water and dangled in mid-air.

"He's massive!" Jake declared excitedly as the fish was unhooked. But without so much as a second glance at it, the fisherman popped it into a keep net half submerged in the canal.

"Will you eat it?" Candy asked, trying not to look disgusted.

"Not me," said the fisherman, wrinkling his nose. "I don't actually like fish. Usually I give them away, or just let them go." He glanced at his watch. It was an expensive-looking gold watch with a gold strap. "Deary me, look at the time!"

Jake and Candy watched as he threw everything into his wicker basket and folded his chair. Almost as a last thought he remembered the keep net and the fish.

Hauling it out of the water, he grabbed the wriggling fish and placed it in Jake's hands.

He smiled a twitchy sort of smile. "There, a nice perch for your supper. Must go. Bye!"

And without another word he practically ran along the towpath back towards the road.

Candy and Jake looked at the fish. Its round, desperate eyes reminded Candy of something – or rather someone. But while Benjamin Fisher didn't belong in the dark murky depths of the canal, the fish did.

Jake was obviously thinking the same thing. Without a word, he knelt down and returned the fish carefully to the water.

With a crooked little smile, he glanced up at Candy and said, "I quite fancy some chips, though."

11

"Ketchup anyone?" the landlady asked, hovering around their table in *The King Edward Inn* that evening.

"Yes, please," said Jake, plopping great dollops of red sauce all over his burger and chips.

Katherine Elizabeth Eastwood, the landlady of *The King Edward*, smiled at Mr Everton. "Glad to see it hasn't put them off their food."

"Nothing puts these two off their food," their dad remarked, tucking into his own steak and chips.

The landlady remained, hovering. Then,

impulsively, she pulled up a stool and sat down beside them.

They stopped eating, forkfuls of food halfway to their mouths. The landlady looked embarrassed and awkward.

"Sorry," she murmured, keeping her voice low, even though there was no one else in the pub. "Only the lad here said he'd found Benjamin's diary."

"Yes?" Candy answered, putting down her fork.

The landlady's cheeks started to turn a darker shade of pink. "Only . . . I just wondered if Kieran or myself are mentioned in it . . . much."

Candy gave Jake a swift glance. "No, not much."

"But we are mentioned . . . a bit?" the landlady pressed, growing pinker by the second.

"Yeah, a bit," shrugged Jake, popping a chunk of burger into his mouth.

The landlady dragged her stool even closer. "What . . . what did Benjamin write?"

"That he had a meal here," Candy answered, studying Katherine Elizabeth Eastwood carefully and wondering if she had the strength to push a big man like Benjamin Fisher over-board, and hold him under till he drowned.

"And that's all?" the landlady asked in disbelief.

"Well, we haven't read all of his diary yet, just bits of it," Candy explained.

The landlady's plump face twitched into a smile, but her eyes were cold. "You know, I don't really think it's very nice, reading someone else's diary. Specially after they're dead."

"I agree whole-heartedly," said Mr Everton, cutting through his steak, then adding, "but rather us than anyone who actually knew him, wouldn't you agree?"

Her smile froze, and without another word she got up and scuttled back behind the bar.

Mr Everton winked. "Got a guilty conscience, has that one."

Candy and Jake were enjoying their banana splits when the pub started to fill up. The landlady had vanished somewhere and her husband was serving behind the bar. Jason Quinn, the runner, was the next customer to come in. He was wearing a track suit this time, with running shoes, although he didn't look like he'd been running.

He walked straight up to the landlord and instantly an unspoken message seemed to pass between them: a questioning look in the landlord's eye, and a brief, almost unnoticeable shake of the runner's head.

Candy and Jake looked at each other.

Almost at once the landlady reappeared from the back room. Just like her husband, she gave Jason Quinn a questioning look. Once again came the brief shake of the head.

"See that?" Jake hissed.

Candy nodded.

"What do you reckon they're up to?"

She shrugged. "I don't know. Unless Jason Quinn was the one who ransacked our boat looking for the diary."

Her dad almost choked. "Now what are you two on about?"

With a brief look at her brother, Candy quietly explained. "We didn't mention it before, Dad, but someone was on the *Baloo* today and went through all the drawers and cupboards."

"What!"

Jake continued, "We reckon whoever it was, was after the diary."

His dad stared in disbelief. "Kids, I'm getting

a bit fed up hearing about this diary. Let's have a look at it."

Candy and Jake didn't make a move.

"Have you got it with you?" demanded Mr Everton.

Jake nodded.

"Let me see it, then."

With a sigh, Jake pulled it from his back pocket.

"Thank you," said his dad, settling back to read it.

Candy tried to get on with her dessert, but now it didn't seem quite so appealing. More interesting was what her dad would have to say after reading Benjamin Fisher's last words.

Suddenly Jake began kicking her foot under the table. She glanced up, and saw his face. His eyes darted in the direction of the three people huddled like conspirators at the bar.

The landlord and landlady and the runner.

They were standing open-mouthed, staring at Kevin Everton reading Benjamin Fisher's diary. The landlady had her hand on her husband's arm, as if restraining him, stopping him from coming over and snatching it from them.

Finally Mr Everton handed the diary back to Jake. "Interesting," was all he said.

"So, what do you think?" Jake hissed as he slipped it into his back pocket, glancing at the three who were still watching.

"I think Benjamin Fisher was a bit of a rogue," said his dad. "And I think he made himself so nervous he slipped and fell overboard. Now then, if you've both finished your meal, shall we go?"

Candy nodded, and glanced sideways to see if they were still being watched.

They were. Or to be precise, Jake was.

12

Walking back to the *Baloo*, Candy had the distinct feeling that hostile eyes were still on them. She glanced back over her shoulder constantly, half expecting someone to be creeping up behind them, ready to snatch the diary from Jake's back pocket.

The sun was sinking fast, casting a deep red glow across the sky, darkening the trees until they were black silhouettes enticing the birds home for the night.

Over the surface of the canal, swarms of gnats gathered in clusters, easy prey for the swooping bats that appeared from nowhere.

"Who's that?" Kevin Everton suddenly murmured.

"Where?"

He pointed to the *Baloo*. "There's someone on our boat!"

He was right. A head was clearly visible near the cabin door. Someone was trying to get in.

"Stay back you two, just in case," Mr Everton murmured, quickening his pace.

Candy and Jake had no intention of staying back, but they had to run to keep up with their dad. They slowed only as they reached the bow of the *Baloo*. Candy gripped Jake's arm, holding him back a little as their dad jumped on board.

"Can I help you?"

The postwoman, Kitty Ellis, practically fell backwards in fright. She grabbed hold of the *Baloo*'s roof to steady herself with one hand. In the other she was holding something. It was a pie.

"Oh, you did give me a fright!" she said, patting her chest to make sure her heart was still beating. "No wonder I couldn't make anyone hear me knocking. You were all out."

"That's right," said Mr Everton. "What can we do for you?"

She smiled. It wasn't the sort of smile that came easily. It looked almost painful. "I just wanted to make amends. I think I was a little bit rude to you when we met this morning. I do hope we can be friends."

Not if you burn any more mail, Candy thought to herself.

Mr Everton smiled and unlocked the galley door. "That's fine by me."

Kitty Ellis held out the peace offering. "It's apple. I thought you might like one."

"That's very kind of you," Mr Everton said, accepting the pie and taking it below deck. "Come on in, won't you?"

The postwoman went down the little steps and looked all around the living quarters. "It looks very spick and span now. It certainly didn't look this tidy when Benjamin was living here."

"I gather you didn't get on with Benjamin very well," said Mr Everton, offering her a seat at the little table.

"Benjamin liked to cause mischief whenever he could. I personally think he took great pleasure in worrying people," she replied stiffly, and then she sighed. "Ah well, it's all water under the bridge now, if you'll pardon the expression."

As the postwoman continued chatting to her dad, Candy watched her closely, wondering if she was Benjamin's murderer. Although she didn't look very strong, she obviously was or she couldn't carry a heavy mail sack around day after day.

Anyway, perhaps she had poisoned the pie first, so that when she eventually pushed Benjamin overboard, he was too weak to struggle.

Mr Everton found a clean knife. "You know, this pie looks absolutely delicious. Apple's my favourite."

"Dad!" Candy cried, her eyes huge.

He raised his eyebrows. "What? I never had pudding like you two. I'm entitled to a piece of pie. Will you join me, Mrs Ellis?"

"Call me Kitty, but no. I really must be getting back." She got to her feet and smiled at them all again. "So nice to have met you all properly. Enjoy the pie."

The second she was gone, Candy grabbed her dad's hand. "Don't eat the pie!" she hissed.

"You've got to be joking," her dad said, looking puzzled.

"It might be poisoned."

"Candy, what are you on about?"

"You never know, she could have poisoned Benjamin's pie so he was dying when she pushed him in and held him down."

Her dad nodded knowingly. "I see. So Kitty Ellis the postwoman murdered Benjamin, did she? I thought the lock-keeper was our culprit."

"It could be either," Jake suggested, breaking a little bit of pie crust off and tasting it. "Mmm, it doesn't taste poisonous."

"Jake, don't!" Candy cried.

Removing Candy's hand from his, Mr Everton proceeded to cut himself a chunk of apple pie. Candy had to admit, it did smell good.

"So what was his last meal? Any clues?" asked their dad.

Candy thought back, her eyes fixed on her dad as he prepared to eat the pie. "There were some old fish bones on a mouldy plate."

"Not pie?"

"Well, she would hardly leave the evidence, would she?" Candy answered, holding her breath as her father bit into the pie.

His eyes closed in delight as he savoured it. Then suddenly, he clutched at his throat. His eyes bulged and horrible gurgling sounds came from his mouth.

"Dad!" Candy and Jake shrieked together.

His expression changed. A big grin crept over his face. "Too much sugar," he joked. And took another bite.

Candy thumped him.

It was dark when they realized they hadn't brought the sleeping-bags and pillows in from the car. Candy and Jake were both in their pyjamas, ready to climb into the bunk beds.

"I'll nip back to the car and fetch them now," their dad said, pulling on his sweater.

"The towpath is going to be awfully dark, Dad, specially in the tunnel. Be careful you don't fall in the canal."

"I'll take my torch. Will you two be all right till I get back?"

"Course we will," Jake shrugged, glancing up from Benjamin Fisher's diary.

"Well, I've pulled the curtains, so it's all nice and cosy down here," said his dad. "I'll be as quick as I can."

Candy smiled and climbed up to the top bunk with the old newspaper. She had decided to read through it again in case she had missed anything.

"Won't be long," her dad said, closing the galley door. Candy and Jake felt the boat dip slightly as he jumped off on to the towpath.

Then there was silence.

Candy glanced up from the newspaper. Down here in the galley of the *Baloo*, it really was cheerful and cosy. With the curtains drawn against the dark, and all the wall lights glowing brightly, it felt snug and safe.

It was hard to think that a murderer was roaming free outside.

Candy tried to imagine how that person would be feeling now. Now that their victim's body had been discovered.

Now that they knew there was a possibility that their motive could be written in Benjamin's diary.

Benjamin's written word could be just as damning as anything he could have said.

And if they had murdered Benjamin to keep him quiet, wouldn't they be just as desperate now to make sure the diary was never made public?

If they'd killed once to hide their guilty secret, what was to stop them from killing again?

"What was that?" Jake hissed suddenly.

Candy had heard it too. Just a slight noise outside their boat. A twig breaking on the towpath.

Only twigs don't just break by themselves. Usually they break when someone steps on one.

Jake was sitting on the top bunk opposite his sister. His eyes looked almost too large for his face in the flickering lamplight. "Take a look," he whispered.

Cautiously Candy moved the edge of a curtain aside and peeped through, but all she could see was her own wide-eyed reflection peering back at her.

"Can't see anything. Maybe it was an animal – a fox or something."

"Shall we go out and see?" Jake whispered.

Candy gasped. "Are you mad?"

"So we just sit and wait?" Jake said sullenly. "And what if it's the murderer lurking about outside? What if it's the three from the pub? They saw Dad reading the diary. They might be waiting to push him in the canal too so he can't tell anyone what he read."

"Jake, don't say that."

"But it might be," Jake said, jumping down from the bunk bed and pulling his jeans and sweater on over his pyjamas. "You stay here if you like but I'm going to take a look outside."

The thought that somebody could be hiding, waiting for their dad to come back along the towpath, stirred Candy into action too. She dragged on her sweater and followed Jake up on to the deck.

They stood by the tiller at the rear of the boat, trying to make out shapes under the moonlight. The night was blacker than any night at home. No street lights or car lights, just the faint glow from the drawn curtains at the inn and the nearby cottages.

Candy squinted and opened her eyes wide, trying to get accustomed to the blackness. Trying to see if any of the shadows were moving.

The soft lapping of the water against the hull of the *Baloo* was the only sound. Occasionally there was a splash as a fish surfaced or a water rat went swimming.

Candy shivered. "Can you see him yet?"

Jake shook his head. "How long should it

take him to walk back to where we left the car? He's been gone ages."

"Ten minutes there, ten minutes back," Candy guessed, straining her eyes in the hope of seeing a glimmer of her dad's torch light.

Suddenly, there was a sound behind them. They both swung round. For a second there was nothing, just the cold blackness of the night.

Then there was a scampering sound and a small Jack Russell terrier came bounding along the towpath from the direction of the pub. Following behind, Candy could make out the large, burly shape of a man.

Her heart thudded and she gripped Jake's arm.

As the shadowy figure came closer, Candy recognized it as the landlord. He looked larger in his jacket and wellingtons.

"Hello! What are you two doing up at this time of night?" he greeted them.

Candy gulped, not sure whether she was relieved to find it was him, or not. "Oh, just getting some fresh air," she lied, not wanting to admit her dad wasn't there.

His small eyes glowed in the moonlight. "Not nervous sleeping in a dead man's bed?"

Pleasantly put, Candy thought grimly. But she smiled confidently. "No, not really. I mean, it wasn't as if he died in his bed. He died out here, didn't he?"

The landlord nodded his large round head vaguely. "He certainly did. Poor old Ben! Funny how someone like him, who'd lived all his life afloat, could be so clumsy as to fall overboard and not be able to drag himself out. Must have drunk himself silly."

"Yeah, he had a big stash of booze," Jake piped up. "Same sort of brandy that Dad was on about in your pub. You know, the stuff you can only buy on the Continent."

Candy dug him in the ribs. The last thing they wanted was to antagonize the landlord. He could have murdered already for all they knew.

While Candy couldn't see his expression clearly, the landlord's voice seemed to have risen an octave. "Yes, well, lots of people travel abroad these days. No law against it," he added jokily.

"Course not," Candy agreed. Although there *was* a law about importing huge quantities of alcohol and selling it in pubs.

The Jack Russell, which had been sniffing and scuffling around at the waterside, suddenly stood to attention, barking at someone coming through the tunnel. Candy swung round and saw the spot of light coming from a torch.

"Looks like your dad's coming back," the landlord announced, and called out, "Good evening, sir. Glad to see you haven't missed your footing and fallen in."

Mr Everton called out something in reply, but Candy wasn't listening. She was wondering how he knew their dad was out. Had he been watching the *Baloo* and seen him go? Was his the footstep outside the *Baloo* that broke the twig?

Mr Everton's head peered out from behind a mountain of sleeping-bags and pillows. "What are you two up to?"

"Just watching for you," Candy answered, frowning, disliking the way the landlord was lending a helpful hand as their dad clambered on board.

Was he really as friendly as he pretended? Or was he just waiting for a chance to push their dad – and anyone else who'd read the diary – into a watery grave?

"Here you go kids," said Mr Everton, dumping the sleeping-bags on to Jake and Candy. "Make yourselves useful. Nice evening," he remarked to the landlord.

Reluctant to leave their unsuspecting dad with the inn landlord, Candy and Jake hurriedly deposited the bedding on the bunks down in the galley.

"He must have seen Dad leave. He must have been watching," Candy murmured anxiously.

But Jake didn't answer. He was staring at the door that led on to the bow – the opposite end to where they had all just been. "This is odd."

"What is?"

Jake gave the door a tiny push and it swung open. "Candy, this door was shut."

"It couldn't have been," Candy frowned. "It must have blown open when we went out the back end."

"It can't blow open. It's got a latch. . ." His words died away and he clambered up on to his bunk and began searching frantically around. "Oh no!"

"What's wrong? Jake, what have you lost?"

"Someone's been in here, Candy," he said knowingly. "For the few minutes we were out there at the back, someone crept in through the front and stole the diary!"

13

"Dad, the diary's gone!" Candy cried as soon as Mr Everton came below deck.

"Well, don't look at me, I gave it back to you," he replied, smoothing his sleeping-bag out and fluffing up his pillow.

"Someone's stolen it!" Candy blurted out. "Someone crept in that door while we were all out at the other end of the boat and stole the diary!"

He raised his eyebrows, unimpressed. "Kids, please. It's late. No doubt we'll come across it in the morning. Now then, shall we try and get some sleep? It's been one heck of a long day."

There was no point arguing, and reluctantly Candy and Jake got into their bunks.

Candy thumped her pillow and glanced across at Jake. "The landlord must have had an accomplice," she whispered. "They must have worked it out. They make a sound so we come out, then he keeps us talking while his wife or the runner nips in and searches for the diary."

"Yeah," agreed Jake. "Only how could they be sure we would come out?"

Candy shrugged. "Don't suppose they were. I think they were just waiting and hoping for a chance, and we provided it."

Jake flung himself flat on his back. "Those creeps!"

"Kids, give it a rest, will you?" Mr Everton interrupted. "You'll be giving yourselves nightmares. Anyway, changing the subject slightly, Jake, I saw a smart-looking car parked up on the main road near ours that you would have been most impressed with."

"Yeah? What was it?" Jake asked enthusiastically.

Candy groaned. Did that really matter when there was a murderer walking loose? When that murderer could have been in their boat not fifteen minutes ago?

But Jake and his dad were now discussing cars.

"Fabulous motor," Mr Everton went on. "Top of the range Mercedes, personalized number plates, the lot. AR1 it was."

Candy closed her eyes. There would be no getting Jake back on to the mystery of the missing diary now. His head would be full of cars and engines and dreams of winning the Grand Prix. She began to drift off to sleep, her dad's words still laying on her mind. Personalized number plates indeed! So pretentious! AR1 – what did that stand for, heaven's sake? Awfully Rich One?

She smiled sleepily. Then suddenly it struck her. She'd seen those initials somewhere before. She'd actually seen them printed somewhere, and it wasn't on a car's number plate.

She could picture them in gold. On a wicker basket.

Of course! The fisherman's initials were AR.

She stared up at the roof. Was that his car parked out on the road? If it was, what was he still doing here? He'd left ages ago. He must have come back, but why?

And if he was still hanging around, maybe *he* had stolen the diary, though she couldn't think why he would want to.

Sleep was the last thing on her mind now, even though the gentle rocking of the boat on the water had a soothing effect on everyone but her, and before long her dad's snores were echoing along the waterway.

Jake was soon sound asleep too and Candy wished she could do the same, but there were too many thoughts flitting about in her head.

Someone had pushed Benjamin Fisher overboard and held him there until he drowned. Possibly their initials were KE, unless KE was the beginning of a word he was trying to write.

Katherine and Kieran Eastwood, the inn keepers of *The King Edward*.

Kitty Ellis the postwoman.

The keeper of the Lock – Ted Johnstone.

Staring once more up at the ceiling, Candy tried to make sense of it all.

If the landlord and landlady of *The King Edward* and the runner, Jason Quinn, were involved in illegal alcohol smuggling and selling with Benjamin, they were obviously worried in case Benjamin had written all about it in his diary. So they had a motive for stealing the diary. But did they have a motive for murdering Benjamin?

Candy tossed and turned in her bed. Why would they want to kill Benjamin if he was helping them with their smuggling racket? He could hardly land them in trouble with the police without getting himself in trouble too.

But what if they were involved in something else illegal? Like a jewellery raid? What if they were the burly intruders who had broken into that jewellery shop in town and stolen a quarter of a million pounds' worth of jewellery? What if Benjamin had found out about that?

That could definitely be a motive for murder!

Then she remembered how the runner had thought Benjamin was back on his boat that morning. If the runner had been involved in his murder, he wouldn't have come looking for Benjamin – unless he was pretending.

It was the same with the pub landlady. She was so upset about Benjamin's death – unless she was pretending too.

Candy sighed. And what about the post-woman? She paid for Benjamin's silence over her burning those letters by giving him apple pies. Was she really so worried he might report her that she murdered him for it?

Then there was the lock-keeper, Ted Johnstone. Had Benjamin threatened to tell everyone that he hadn't completed fifty years' perfect service? Was Ted Johnstone such a proud man that he would kill to keep his reputation intact?

Candy moaned to herself. It might be any one of them. There was no point in trying to guess. She would have to look at the facts.

Sitting up in her bunk, she found herself a notepad and pencil. In neat handwriting, she wrote down some ideas.

For a murder you needed:

1 Motive – a very good reason for wanting that person dead.

2 The opportunity to commit the murder without being seen.

3 The ability to kill someone. Benjamin was a big man. Either his killer was stronger than him, or Benjamin had been weakened first.

4 A victim – Benjamin.

5 A murderer – ?

Next she listed all the people connected with Benjamin:

Ted Johnstone, the lock-keeper.
Kitty Ellis, the postwoman.
Katherine Elizabeth Eastwood, landlady of *The King Edward Inn*.
Kieran Eastwood, landlord of *The King Edward*.
Jason Quinn, runner.

She thought for a second about the fisherman. He knew Benjamin too, only she wasn't aware of any guilty secret there, although he had been so nervous and jumpy.

Candy read her list again. If her guesses were correct, all of those people had a guilty secret which Benjamin knew about, and could have been blackmailing them over.

In other words, they all had a motive.

They all had the opportunity to murder Benjamin too, as it had happened in the middle of the night on a dark, lonely canal.

But did they all have the *ability* to push him overboard and hold him down?

Candy put a tick next to the names of Ted

Johnstone, Kieran Eastwood, and Jason Quinn. They were all big and strong.

She put a question mark next to the landlady and the postwoman.

Next, she got the old newspaper out and spread it across her bunk. Whatever had triggered Benjamin's murder, it was connected with something he'd read in this newspaper.

She listed all the names she recognized:

Katherine Elizabeth Eastwood.
Kieran Eastwood.
Jason Quinn.

She sighed. Those news stories referred to pleasant things: a wedding, someone being lorry driver of the year. Nothing there to get Benjamin so excited that he would try to blackmail someone over it.

Candy scratched her head. It just had to be connected with the jewellery theft. What was it Benjamin had written? *Beats me why people do these naughty little crimes if they don't like being found out.*

The jewellery theft had taken place right here

in town, and the owner had been robbed by two burly intruders.

Candy frowned as she re-read the story. Arthur Rathbone, the jeweller, had tried to fight off the intruders using his martial arts skills.

Arthur Rathbone . . . the name rang a bell again. Where on earth had she heard that name? Arthur R – AR.

Her eyes popped. AR! The initials on the fisherman's wicker basket and on his posh car's number plate!

Of course! Yesterday, when the police were taking everyone's names and addresses, one of the policemen had known him. He'd asked how he was enjoying his retirement.

Candy glanced back at the story and read:

"It's all very upsetting," Mr Rathbone told our reporter. "Makes me think it's time to retire from the jewellery trade. . ."

No wonder the fisherman was so nervous and jumpy! He'd already had one really bad experience when he was robbed of all his jewellery. Then to find one of his friends had drowned! Poor man!

Nevertheless, she picked up her pencil and neatly added Arthur Rathbone, fisherman, to her list of suspects.

"What are you doing?" Jake murmured sleepily, opening one eye.

"Trying to work out who killed Benjamin."

"Probably the same person who sneaked in here and nicked the diary," Jake whispered, so as not to wake his dad.

Candy shrugged. "Not necessarily. Lots of people wanted to read what Benjamin had written about them, but only one person killed him."

"Could have been more than one," Jake suggested. "Like those three at the pub."

"Yes, I realize that, but I can't help thinking it's got something to do with the jewellery theft." She smiled then. "Oh yes, something else – I think the fisherman is called Arthur Rathbone, who was the owner of the jewellery shop."

Jake opened his other eye. "Yeah?"

"Maybe," continued Candy thoughtfully, "maybe Benjamin saw the robbers hiding the jewels and maybe he said he'd tell on them unless they gave him some."

"Not a good idea," Jake murmured.

"No," agreed Candy. "They were two burly intruders. It could have been the landlord and his wife, or Jason Quinn. Or even Ted Johnstone."

Jake began to chuckle. "Hey, what if it was that old couple from the shop? Bonny and Clyde in disguise!"

Candy burst out laughing and her dad turned in his sleep and snored loudly.

"Sshh!" muttered Jake.

Candy tried to stop herself laughing, but she could still picture the little old couple with a machine-gun in one hand and a bag of humbugs in the other.

Mr Everton stirred again and Candy buried her face in her pillow.

Suddenly there was a sound. Her laughter stopped. It had come from just outside their boat.

Heavy boots scuffing on the rutted towpath. The distinct sound of heavy breathing.

Candy went icy cold.

"Jake!"

Jake was still chuckling. "Do you reckon they made their getaway on stolen zimmer frames?"

"Jake! Listen!"

"What?"

"There's someone outside."

14

Not moving, scarcely daring to breathe, they listened. Whoever it was, they were pacing alongside the *Baloo*. First one way, then the other.

Then the footsteps stopped directly beside Candy's window.

She could practically *feel* the presence of someone. So close. Just centimetres away.

And then, to her horror, she heard the squeak-squeak of a hand rubbing against her window pane, trying to see inside.

Candy couldn't move, she was so scared. Couldn't shout to wake her dad. All she could do was sit rigid, her eyes huge, heart pounding.

Jake had turned white.

Slowly the footsteps dragged themselves along to the rear of the boat. Suddenly it dipped as someone stepped aboard. Candy could feel the *Baloo* tugging gently at its moorings.

A terrifying thought struck her. What if there were such things as ghosts? What if, because they had disturbed Benjamin Fisher's watery grave, he had come back to take over the *Baloo* again?

What if that was Benjamin at the door now: a dead, water-logged, decomposed Benjamin Fisher?

The latch on the door suddenly lifted and Candy's eyes flew to the top bolt, infinitely relieved to see that her dad had drawn it across before getting into bed.

Panic-stricken she reached across the door at her end of the boat and double-checked it was secure, then cried, "Dad!"

"Dad!" Jake joined in, finding his voice and shouting at the top of it.

Mr Everton sat up so quickly he hit his head on the bunk above. "Yow! What . . . who. . .?"

"Someone's trying to get in," Candy cried, jumping down off her bunk and shaking her dad properly awake.

Rubbing his head, he frowned and squinted. "You're dreaming."

"Look for yourself then!" she cried, pointing at the latch clattering on its hook.

Mr Everton swung out of bed. "Who the devil is that?"

"Be careful," Candy whispered, creeping along the galley after him.

Picking up Benjamin's half-painted kettle as a weapon, Mr Everton inched towards the door. "Stay back," he hissed. Then, sliding back the bolt, he pulled the door open.

Ted Johnstone, the lock-keeper, stood there, blocking the moonlight with his bulk. He looked, thought Candy, larger than life standing there at the top of the little galley stairs, looking down at them with hard, sharp eyes.

"Mr Johnstone!" gasped Mr Everton. "What are you doing here?"

"Sorry to disturb you," he said in a hushed voice, as if he didn't want anyone else to know he was there. Not that there was anyone else around as far as Candy knew. He went on, "I wouldn't bother you if it wasn't an emergency. Thing is, some folk have got themselves in a lot of trouble further up the canal. Their boat's well and truly wedged and is in danger of capsizing if we don't get it sorted pretty quickly."

"At this time of night? It's – " Mr Everton glanced at his watch – "one o'clock in the morning!"

"Aye, it seems they've been struggling for hours. Folk on holiday. Haven't a clue how to handle a narrowboat. They've just knocked on my door and asked for help. I've taken a look, but I can't do it on my own. Need a few pairs of strong hands. I've enlisted the help of another couple of chaps. I'd appreciate it if you could lend a hand too, sir."

"Well . . . yes, I suppose, so," Mr Everton agreed, much to Candy and Jake's dismay.

"Dad, you're not going out now, are you?" Candy asked anxiously.

"You heard what the man said – someone needs help." He hurried to the bunk end of the boat and dressed quickly. "You'll be all right, won't you? Stay put, lock the doors and get back to sleep."

Candy watched helplessly as he tied his shoes. In a tiny voice she whispered, "Dad, I don't trust him. I don't think you should go off with him."

Mr Everton smiled. "Candy, how would you feel if we were in trouble and no one came to help? Now don't fret. I'll be back before you know it."

Ruffling her hair and Jake's, he pulled on his jacket and joined the lock-keeper out on the towpath.

"Lock that door now, kids," he called, as he and Ted Johnstone strode off along the towpath and disappeared into the night.

Candy turned anxiously to her brother. "Jake, I don't like this."

Jake's face looked white under the moonlight. "Neither do I."

There was no point in trying to get to sleep. Both of them knew that it would be impossible until their dad was safely back. But as the minutes ticked by, they began to wonder if that would ever happen.

"What if it was a trick?" Jake asked unhappily as they sat on their bunk beds, staring at the floor. "What if the lock-keeper murdered

Benjamin, and now he's going to murder us in case we've discovered his guilty secret too?"

"Don't say that, Jake," Candy murmured, trying not to imagine Ted Johnstone pushing their dad into the canal and holding him down until he drowned, before coming after them. He was so big. Would their dad be stronger? She didn't know. She just didn't know. "I'm sure Ted Johnstone is a perfectly nice person," she went on, trying to convince herself as well as Jake. "I mean, he's spent all his life working on the canals, making sure everyone stays safe. He's not going to become a mass murderer now . . . is he?"

"I hope not," Jake answered shakily. "What was that?"

Candy's heart lurched. "Oh, stop it, Jake. I'm nervous enough."

"I heard a splash. Didn't you hear it?"

"It was probably just a duck or something," Candy said, determined not to get hysterical about this. She opened her notebook. "I was trying to work it out logically. I've made a list of suspects, motives and opportunities."

Jake's eyes were wide. "There it is again! A glooping sound, like something being dropped into the canal."

"Jake, don't!"

"Candy, I heard something."

Sighing, she closed her notebook. "Jake, if you're just winding me up. . ."

"I'm not," he wailed.

She jumped off the bunk bed. "Come on then, let's go and check."

Jake followed. "If we turn the lights off we'll be able to look out the door without anyone seeing us."

At the click of a switch they were plunged into darkness. Jake instantly banged his toe on something and moaned.

"Sshh!"

They inched towards the galley door at the bow of the boat and softly drew back the bolt and lifted the latch. The door creaked on its hinges as Candy slowly pulled it open. Pale moonlight flooded in, so that when they looked out over the canal, it seemed almost illuminated, bathed in starlight.

They immediately saw what was making the glooping sounds.

"The fisherman!" hissed Jake.

"Arthur Rathbone! What's he doing fishing at this time of night?"

"Yeah, specially when he doesn't even like fish."

Candy frowned. "Dad said his car was parked out on the road when he went to fetch the sleeping-bags. He must have been in the pub all evening, because he wasn't out fishing when we were talking to the landlord."

Jake's eyes shifted accusingly. "We didn't *see* him earlier, but obviously he was around somewhere. So maybe it was him who sneaked in and stole the diary."

"Why would he do that?" Candy asked, puzzled, watching the fisherman as he busied himself on the canal bank, unaware that they were watching him. "Benjamin couldn't have been blackmailing him. Poor old Arthur Rathbone was a victim himself. He's had all his jewellery stolen and he's had to retire."

Jake looked unimpressed. "He hasn't done badly on it though, has he? Posh car, expensive watch, flashy rings, gold teeth."

"Well no, I suppose he hasn't," agreed Candy. "But it must have been awful getting robbed."

"He would have been insured," said Jake, closing the door and putting the light back on.

Candy opened the newspaper and scanned the article. "Actually, Jake, you're right. It says here that he was insured."

"Yeah. Those robbers did him a favour if you ask me."

A thought struck Candy suddenly. "Jake, what if he knew the robbers? What if he put them up to it?"

Jake's eyes popped. "And Benjamin overheard them discussing it!"

Another thought struck Candy. Softly, she murmured, "Or . . . what if there were no robbers at all? What if Arthur Rathbone stole his own jewellery, made up a story about being robbed, and claimed on the insurance?"

Jake whistled. "Yeah, that's a pretty good reason for Benjamin to try and blackmail him. And a good reason to keep him quiet."

Candy opened her notebook and put a tick beside the fisherman's name. "Well, he might have a motive, if he is a crook. But if he's not and really did get robbed, then we can cross him off." She groaned. "Except he's only a little chap. Benjamin was twice his size. He wouldn't be able to push Benjamin overboard and hold him under. He's not strong enough."

Jake climbed on to Candy's bunk. "So what have we got?"

Candy started to go through all the suspects once more, but she felt as if she were going round in circles. Finally, she pushed her notebook aside and sighed.

"Oh, I don't know! Jake, it could be anyone. I give up!"

But Jake took the notebook off her and opened it again. "We can't give up, Candy."

"Why can't we?"

Jake looked steadily at her. His expression was deadly serious. "Because . . ." he began softly . . . "our lives might depend on us working out who the killer is – before he kills us!"

15

"So," began Candy, trying not to yawn, "we reckon Benjamin was murdered by someone he was blackmailing. So who had a guilty secret that he knew about?"

Jake reeled off the list of suspects. "The lock-keeper, the landlord and landlady, the runner, the postwoman, and possibly the fisherman."

"Right," said Candy, scribbling them down. "Then our next clue is the initials KE. So that's the lock-keeper, Kieran and Katherine Eastwood and Kitty Ellis."

"Don't write our dad's name on that list," Jake muttered.

Candy glared at him. "I wasn't going to!"

"What else do we have to consider?" asked Jake. "I know. Out of that lot, who is physically capable of pushing someone as big and strong as Benjamin into the water and holding him down?"

Candy sighed. "I think we can cross off the postwoman, the landlady and the fisherman."

"So who are we left with?" asked Jake, peering at her list. "Ah-ha! The landlord Kieran Eastwood and the lock-keeper. I reckon it's the landlord because he was around when the diary went missing."

"So he must be working with someone else. He didn't have a chance to nip on to the *Baloo*, but his accomplice could have while he kept us occupied."

"And that has to be his wife or the runner," said Jake. "Only I'm not sure because the landlady was so upset that Benjamin was dead, and the runner thought Benjamin was back on his boat this morning, remember?"

Candy nodded. "They could both have been pretending."

"I still think the landlord is in this," said Jake. "He's the most likely of our suspects."

Candy nodded sleepily. "I know, he's our best suspect and it still might not be him. So, let's look at the least likely suspect."

"The postwoman?" Jake suggested. "She's not mentioned in the paper. Benjamin was only blackmailing her for apple pies, and she's not strong enough to drown him. It's definitely her!"

"She could have drugged or poisoned the pie first?"

Jake just looked at her then shook his head. "Nah!"

They sat quietly, thinking. Outside, the glooping sound continued. Finally Candy said, "What *is* he doing? Sounds like he's dropping something heavy into the water, like that huge magnet of his." Her eyes widened. "I bet he's dropped his car keys in. Maybe that's why his car's been here all evening. He dropped his keys in and he's been fishing for them off and on all night."

Jake pulled a face. "What an idiot! I mean, if you drop your keys into the canal so often that you have to carry a massive big magnet with you which must weigh a tonne, why not do something simpler and lighter – like attaching your keys to a block of wood, like Dad did? You drop them in and they float."

Candy shrugged. "We could go and ask him, only I reckon he would jump out of his skin if we crept up on him in the dark."

"He's a bit of a weed," Jake agreed, grinning.

"I know, and we're not looking for a weed, are we?" Candy murmured quietly. "We're looking for someone strong enough to kill a man."

"The landlord, the lock-keeper or the runner," supplied Jake.

Candy continued. "Someone with the initials KE."

"The landlord and the lock-keeper," said Jake.

"Someone with a reason to kill."

Jake thought for a while. Then, with a deadly seriously look, he said, "The lock-keeper is a proud man. He likes people to think he's wonderful. He's due to be rewarded for his long service to the waterways soon. Just think how his pride would be dented if people knew he was in charge when a child drowned in his lock – even if it was years ago. I think it could be him, Candy. I think it could be the lock-keeper."

A cold shiver ran down Candy's spine as she recalled how the lock-keeper had stared down at Benjamin's body in the water. How satisfied he'd looked.

Yes, it was possible, she realized. There was something sinister about Ted Johnstone the lock-keeper. Perhaps he *was* the murderer. It was a horrifying thought.

But there was something even more horrifying to consider. And in a tiny whisper, she voiced her fears to Jake. Softly she murmured, "And he's taken our dad. . ."

16

Candy desperately wanted to go out and look for her dad and the lock-keeper, but her head was spinning. She sat for a few minutes, cross-legged on her bunk bed, staring at the notepad. Trying to make sense of it all.

You had to have a very strong reason for murdering someone. Benjamin was murdered because he had tried to blackmail someone over something they had done.

Something that only *he* knew about.

If it was common knowledge, then the murderer would have to kill everyone who knew.

So this had to be a guilty secret that only Benjamin and the murderer knew about.

A tingle ran down her spine. She thought of all the guilty secrets which the people had around here. The lock-keeper's secret of the child who drowned was known by the old couple in the shop.

The postwoman's guilty secret of burning the mail was known by the runner.

The smuggled booze was known by the landlord, his wife and the runner – and probably all the pub landlords along the canal.

So there had to be another secret. Something *very* secret. Something worth killing over.

Wishing she still had the diary, Candy thought back over the bits she could remember. Then she re-read the newspaper article.

Suddenly, it all slipped into place.

If she and Jake were right about one thing, then everything else fitted perfectly!

Almost perfectly. There was still one thing she didn't understand. Unless. . .

She jumped off the bed and looked at the last painting Benjamin ever did. *A picture paints a thousand words*, Benjamin had written in his diary. It certainly did!

"Jake!" Candy breathed. "Jake . . . I know who murdered Benjamin. And now I know why!"

He stared at her. "Who?"

She picked up her notebook. Slowly, she drew a circle around the name of the suspect. Jake's eyes widened. "Are you sure?"

"Positive, and if you want to know why, take a look at this." And she turned the bright red kettle around so Jake could see the picture Benjamin had painted.

"A picture paints a thousand words," Candy murmured. "Benjamin painted what he saw. See? This was his reason for blackmail. We were right!"

Jake blinked. "Of course – KE – it all fits! Candy, what are we going to do?"

She turned off the boat lights. "We'll have to move quickly, Jake. There's not a second to lose."

Grabbing a torch, Candy and Jake tiptoed out into the black night air. They had gone just a few metres along the towpath when they saw their escape route blocked by the very person Benjamin had painted on his kettle.

The killer!
The face looked evil in the pale moonlight.
The voice was a cold, unpleasant whisper.
"Going somewhere, children?"

17

"For the police," Candy said bravely, gripping Jake's arm.

The smile looked cunning in the darkness. "So you've worked it out. I should congratulate you. Benjamin must have written all about it in his diary. What a shame I didn't get the diary off you sooner! I was just coming for it now."

Candy glanced at her brother, then back at the killer. "It's gone. If you didn't take it, someone else with a guilty conscience did first."

"Only they weren't as guilty as you!" Jake raged, his voice carrying on the silent air.

Then, without any warning of what he was going to do, Jake charged forward, giving Benjamin's killer an almighty push.

Taken by surprise, and caught off balance, the killer toppled backwards into the cold, murky canal.

There was a huge splash.

Candy grabbed Jake. "Brilliant! Now run, Jake. Run as fast as you can!"

They raced along the narrow footpath into the pitch black tunnel.

"There's a phone box near where we left the car," Candy gasped, her voice echoing around the damp, brick archway. "We'll call the police from there."

Emerging from the darkness into the moonlight, they finally reached the phone box and with trembling fingers Candy dialled nine, nine, nine. "Keep watching, Jake," she gasped, before blurting out the whole story to the police.

They waited, trembling, on the roadside until the sound of police sirens filled the night. Three police cars screamed to a halt and the officers, one with a police dog, leapt out.

"That way!" Candy shouted, pointing along

the towpath. As Candy and Jake raced after the officers they could hear the sounds of big heavy boots thudding and echoing through the tunnel.

Not surprisingly the killer had clambered out of the canal, but the police dog was quick in following the muddy trail. It wasn't long before Benjamin Fisher's murderer was cornered and captured.

Candy and Jake stood a little way off, trembling now from head to foot. As the killer was led away, it all seemed so obvious. There was one thing – one simple thing which they had missed. Something which should have told them straight away.

Candy glanced at her brother. "Jake, I was just thinking about—"

"I know," he nodded. "I didn't give it a second thought either."

Inspector Meade came over to them and patted them both on the back. "Well done, kids. If it wasn't for you two, we would have assumed Benjamin Fisher just fell overboard and drowned."

Candy and Jake shrugged modestly.

"Actually," said Candy, "it's Jake we have to thank really. He did a great shoulder-charge."

"Yeah," said Jake, grinning. "But you worked it all out, Candy."

"Teamwork," the Inspector announced. "That's what it was. And between the pair of you, you captured a killer. Well done!"